WILLIAM AND THE WITCH

WILLIAM LOWERED HIS LENGTH OF STRING. (*See page* 99)

WILLIAM
AND THE WITCH

by
RICHMAL CROMPTON

Illustrated by
THOMAS HENRY *and* HENRY FORD

LONDON
GEORGE NEWNES LIMITED
TOWER HOUSE, SOUTHAMPTON STREET
LONDON, W.C. 2

First Published *1964*

Printed in Great Britain by
Cox & Wyman, Ltd., London, Fakenham and Reading

CONTENTS

For Paul Ashbee

I

WILLIAM THE PSYCHIATRIST

WILLIAM walked slowly and dejectedly down the road. It was not often that William felt dejected, but occasionally a sense of the futility of his life swept over him.

"Here I am," he muttered, "gettin' older an' older every year an' done nothin' yet to make the world ring with my name. Gosh! I haven't even *started*. I bet Christopher Columbus was thinkin' out how to discover America when he was my age. I bet that Watt man that invented steam had started boilin' kettles. There's not much time left. I've got to start soon."

His mind ran over the careers that he had at various times decided to embrace—engine driver, explorer, spy, detective, prime minister, space traveller, sweet shop proprietor, speed-track racer, lion tamer. postman, diver. Somehow the magic was gone from all of them. He had, in imagination, faced such desperate hazards, secured such resounding glory in each that their possibilities seemed to have been exhausted. He had recently found his career as a diver particularly engrossing. Encased in his diver's suit, with mask and breathing tube, he had rifled sunken ships, carried on desperate fights with sharks, whales and sea serpents, and even met and routed, single-handed, a hitherto undiscovered tribe of savages that lived in caves on the floor of the ocean bed. But he had become bored even with these exploits.

"I'm goin' to try somethin' new," he said, his scowling gaze fixed on his shoes as he kicked a stone from one side of the road to the other. "Somethin' I've never tried before. An' I *bet* I get famous at it."

It was lunch-time when he reached home, and still no idea had occurred to him. Sunk in gloomy contemplation, he demolished a large helping of shepherd's pie and was half way through a large helping of rice pudding when his attention was arrested by something that Robert was saying.

"He's taken a house in Green Lane in Marleigh. He's a famous Harley Street psychiatrist, you know. Arnold Summers. Anyone who knows anything about psychiatry knows the name."

"About what?" said William.

"Psychiatry," said Robert shortly, "and don't talk with your mouth full."

"I've never understood quite what they do," said Mrs. Brown.

"They cure mental trouble," said Robert. "I once met a man who'd been to one and he was completely cured."

"But what do they *do*?" said Mrs. Brown.

"Well, as far as I can make out," said Robert, "the patient lies on a couch and talks and the psychiatrist writes down what he says and—well, that seems to cure the whole trouble."

"How very odd!" said Mrs. Brown.

William had stopped eating and was fixing an earnest gaze on Robert.

"What did you say they were called?" he said.

"Psychiatrists," said Robert.

"An' is that all they do?"

"Yes."

"An'—an' they get *famous* jus' doin' that?"

"Yes," snapped Robert. "Stop asking idiotic questions."

"And get on with your lunch, dear," said Mrs. Brown.

William finished his rice pudding hurriedly and in silence, and went out to find Ginger. He found Ginger in his back garden. He had placed an apple on the top of the fence and was aiming at it with his bow and arrow.

"I want to get as good as that William Tell man," he explained. "I thought I'd better practise on the fence before I started on yumans."

"I bet you wouldn't find any yumans to let you start on 'em," said William. "How many times have you hit it, anyway?"

"I haven't counted," said Ginger evasively.

"Well, come along to the ole barn," said William. "I've got somethin' a jolly sight more int'restin' than that for us to do."

"All right," agreed Ginger, who was getting tired of missing his apple.

They set off down the road towards the old barn.

"I've thought of a diff'rent thing I'm goin' to be," said William. "It's goin' to be easier to be famous at than the others."

"What is it?" said Ginger.

"It's——" began William, then stopped short. "Gosh! I've forgotten the word. Anyway, it's curin' mental troubles."

"Oh," said Ginger.

"An' I'm goin' to cure yours, to start with, then you can cure mine. It'll give us a bit of practice."

"How d'you do it?" said Ginger.

"Easy as easy," said William. "You jus' lie down an' talk an' I write it down in a note-book—I've forgot to bring the note-book, but I don't expect it matters. Then I lie down an' talk an'—an'—well, it cures us of mental troubles."

"Oh," said Ginger. "Sounds a bit queer."

"Yes, but it's all *right*," William assured him earnestly. "Robert told me about it an' he knows someone that's had it done, so it mus' be all right. An' this man that's come to live at Marleigh, he does it an' he's got *famous* doin' it. Anyway, you can't get into a mess with it same as you can with the other things—spies an' space travellers an' detectives an' things."

"Yes," said Ginger, his mind going over the disasters that had resulted from some of William's former careers. "You got in a mess over *those* all right."

"Well, I can't over this," said William. "You couldn't get in a mess jus' listenin' to people talkin', nobody could. I wish I'd known about it before. I wouldn't have wasted all that time over detectin' an' space-explorin' an' all the rest of 'em." They entered the doorway of the old barn. "Now come on. You lie down . . . Here's a place for you to lie down."

Ginger inspected it without enthusiasm.

"Why've I got to lie down?"

"'Cause they do," said William impatiently. "You can't get cured of mental troubles standin' up. Gosh! You ought to know that."

"All right," said Ginger, lowering himself on to the floor and watching William suspiciously. "You're not goin' to start ticklin' me, are you?"

Ginger was the only one of the four Outlaws who was ticklish.

"'Course not," said William. "I'm jus' goin' to listen to you talkin'. Go on. Talk."

"What about?" said Ginger.

"Anythin'," said William. "Go on. Start talkin'."

Ginger gave a sudden chuckle.

"That time you started off explorin' in a boat—d'you remember?—an' you thought you'd got to a desert island an' it turned out to be the same place you'd started from!"

"Well, anyone'd have thought it was a desert island. It looked like one."

"It couldn't have."

"It did."

"It didn't."

"It' did."

"It didn't."

"Shut up!"

"Shut up yourself!" said Ginger, rising pugnaciously from his recumbent position.

William pushed him down again.

"They don't do that," he said. "You've got to stay there an' go on talkin'."

"All right," said Ginger. "An' that time you were bein' a detective an' thought that old man had murdered the other old man 'cause you saw him diggin' a hole in the garden an' then it turned out the other old man had only gone away for a holiday. You got in a jolly big mess over that."

"I did *not*," said William heatedly. "An' I bet anyone out of Scotland Yard would have thought he was
a murderer. It was jolly clever of me. An' I *didn't* get
in a mess over it."

"You did!"

"I didn't!"

"You did."

"Oh, shut up an' go on talkin'."

"I am talkin', aren't I?"

"Well, talk a bit of sense . . . Listen! What about
that time I caught that smuggler? I didn't get in a
mess over that."

"You didn't know he was a smuggler. It was an
accident, you catchin' him."

"Gosh! it was my cunnin', pretendin' I didn't know
he was a smuggler."

"It wasn't. You were gettin' up a rebellion an' you
caught him by mistake."

"You don't know what you're talkin' about. You're
crackers."

"I'm not."

"You are."

This time Ginger rose to his feet and the two had a
spirited wrestling match, then sat down side by side
to recover their breath.

"D'you feel any mental trouble?" said William at
last.

"No," said Ginger after a moment's consideration.

"I've cured you, then," said William triumphantly.
"I knew I'd make a jolly good—I wish I could remember the word. I'll find out when I get home an' we'll
start it tomorrow. We'll charge threepence each."

"They won't pay that much," said Ginger.

"They might," said William. "I bet it's less than that man in Harley Street charges. If we could get enough of them we could buy that helicopter."

The helicopter had appeared yesterday in the window of the village shop.

"It was smashing, wasn't it?" went on William. "You jus' fixed that little handle in an' pulled the string an' off it went right up into the air jus' like a real one."

"It was five shillings," said Ginger. "We'd need a jolly lot of them to get five shillings."

"How many?" said William.

It took them several minutes and a series of heated arguments to arrive at the sum.

"Twenty . . ." said William. He looked a little thoughtful for a moment, then recovered his usual optimism. "Well—gosh! There ought to be twenty people about with mental troubles. Twenty's not all that much. I'll find out the word and bring the notice along tomorrow morning."

William brought the notice along the next morning.

"I asked my mother what that word was an' wrote it down soon as she told me," said William. "It's a jolly good notice. We ought to get a lot of people."

He took a drawing pin from his pocket, removed his shoe to act as a hammer and fixed the notice to the door of the old barn.

WILLIAM BROWN

SEKKITRIST

MENTAL TRUBBLES KURED.

THREPPENCE EECH.

"There!" he said proudly. "I bet that's as good as

WILLIAM BROWN
SEKKITRIST
MENTAL TRUBBLES KURED
THREPPENCE EECH

"WHICH OF YOU IS THE PSYCHIATRIST?" ASKED THE HARASSED-
LOOKING MAN.

the one in Harley Street any day. I'll sit on the packin'
case. I'm the one that does it an' you're the recep-
tionist same as at the dentist's. Look out an' see if
anyone's comin'."

Ginger went to the door and looked out.

"There's a man comin' along, takin' the short cut
to the station," he said.

William joined him at the door. A small thin man

with a thin harassed-looking face was making his way across the field.

"Come back into the barn," said William. "I bet the ones in Harley Street don't stand at the door lookin' out for them."

They retired to the inner recesses of the barn.

"He's goin' past," said Ginger.

The man had almost passed the barn when he saw the notice. He stopped to read it, went on a few yards, hesitated, then returned to read it again. Again he went on a few yards, stopped, hesitated, then turned back and entered the barn.

"Which of you is the psychiatrist?" he said, looking from Ginger to William.

"Me," said William. "It's me that cures mental troubles. Have you got any?"

"Yes," said the man. "How do you cure them?"

"You lie down an' talk an' I listen," said William. "There's a dry place over there. 'Least, it was dry yesterday, but it's rained a bit in the night."

"Do you mind if I sit?" said the man, taking his seat on the packing-case. "My name's Peaslake."

"Oh . . ." said William. "Well, I'm William an' he's Ginger. I've not got a note-book 'cause I don't write as quick as people talk. I don't see any sense in a note-book anyway."

"No," said Mr. Peaslake. His face creased into a tight smile that looked even more worried than his frown. "It's utterly ridiculous, of course, my coming in here like this, but I had a letter this morning that's driven me nearly mad. I haven't any intimate friends to confide in and, when I saw your notice, I thought that if I could talk about it to anyone at all it might help."

"All right," said William. "Go on. Talk. Who was this letter from?"

"Amanda. My fiancée," said Mr. Peaslake, fixing his eyes gloomily in front of him. "At least, she *was* my fiancée, but in this letter I've just received she breaks off the engagement. She's coming this evening to return my presents. She has to come in person with her car because one of them's a spin dryer and she can't very well post it. I thought she'd be pleased with the spin dryer, but she said it showed a lack of imagination. She said that all my presents showed a lack of imagination. I knew, of course, that she found me—disappointing in many ways. She says I lack the vital spark. But this letter—well, it's shattered my world to its foundations. I realise that I'm not worthy of her—she's so vibrant and alive—but I simply can't face life without her."

"Well, I think you're jolly lucky gettin' rid of her," said William. "They're all bossy. Gosh! Even when they seem all right at first, they always turn out bossy before they've finished an' they get bossier an' bossier an' bossier. I once knew a girl that——"

"I thought I was supposed to do the talking," put in Mr. Peaslake with his tight smile.

"All right. Go on," said William, abandoning his theme with reluctance. "Go on. Talk."

"Well, there doesn't seem to be any more to say," said Mr. Peaslake. "My whole life's shattered. She's not a woman to act lightly. She's weighed me in the balance and found me wanting. I simply can't face life without her."

"You said that before," said William.

"And I shall probably say it again," said Mr. Peaslake

mournfully. "I know I'm unworthy of her, but I was prepared to spend the rest of my life making myself more worthy."

William was tiring of the subject.

"You've had three-pennyworth of talk about that," he said.

"Well, there's little more to be said," said Mr. Peaslake, heaving a deep sigh.

"Are your mental troubles cured?" said William.

"No," said Mr. Peaslake. He rose from the packing-case. "They're only just beginning. My whole life is shattered to its foundations. Existence will be meaningless from now on." He raised a hand to his head. "I've had the most splitting headache ever since I received the letter."

"It'll be another threepence if you're goin' to start on headaches," William warned him.

"Oh, well . . ." Mr. Peaslake sighed again, took three pennies from his pocket and handed them to William. "Thank you for giving me so much of your time. At least it's wiled away some minutes from the endless stretch of meaningless existence that lies ahead of me."

He gave another deep sigh and set across the field.

"Crackers!" said William. "He jolly well deserves his mental troubles. And serve him right if she took him back, too."

"Someone else is comin'," said Ginger.

Mr. Summers, the well-known psychiatrist, was walking slowly down the hill. Though a well-known psychiatrist, he felt himself to be badly in need of psychiatric treatment. He had tried to treat himself without success, and a streak of mingled pride and obstinacy prevented his going for treatment to another practitioner. Like Mr. Peaslake, he had almost passed the barn door before he saw the notice. Like Mr. Peaslake, he stopped, went on, hesitated, then finally entered the barn.

"Do you want to be done?" said William.

"Yes, please," said Mr. Summers.

He was a short, rather plump man, with a round, fresh-coloured face and thick dark hair.

"Have you got mental trouble?" said William.

"Yes," said Mr. Summers.

"THERE SEEMS TO BE NO COLOUR IN MY LIFE. I'M JUST BORED WITH EVERYTHING."

"They're threepence each," said William. "I mean, if you've got two it's sixpence."

"Fair enough," said Mr. Summers. "What do I do?"

"You're s'posed to lie down, but you can sit if you'd rather. The last one we did sat."

"I'll sit," said Mr. Summers, taking his seat on the packing-case after a cursory glance at the ground. "What do I do now?"

"Talk," said William, "but, if it's about someone shatterin' your life, you needn't say it more than once."

"It isn't," said Mr. Summers. "My trouble is that I'm bored. I've never been bored in my life before, but for the last few months I've been bored to distraction. Things never used to get on my nerves, but now everything gets on my nerves. I thought that a change of surroundings and a temporary move to the country might cure me, so I took a house in this neighbourhood that would enable me to get to and from my work in London. It's a delightful little house in Green Lane over at Marleigh, but everything in it gets on my nerves—the white paint, the cretonne-covered chairs, even the holly bush in the garden. I used to get fun out of everything, even people slipping on banana skins —particularly people slipping on banana skins—but I can't get any fun out of anything now. I feel that if I could have one good belly-laugh I'd be cured, but I can't. There seems to be no colour in my life. I'm bored. I'm just bored with everything."

He stopped.

"Well, go on," said William.

"That's all," said Mr. Summers.

"Are you cured?" said William.

"No," said Mr. Summers.

"Well, it's your fault if you're not," said William, irritated by this second failure. "You can't have talked right."

"Maybe," agreed Mr. Summers.

He rose from the packing case, took out a wallet from his pocket and handed William a ten-shilling note.

"Keep the change," he said, and set off down the field towards the road.

William and Ginger stood staring incredulously at the ten-shilling note.

"Crumbs!" gasped William. "Ten *shillings*!"

"We can get that helicopter now," said Ginger. "We can get *two*. We can get one each."

"Yes, but we've got to *do* somethin' for it," said William. "Gosh, we've *got* to cure his mental troubles now he's given us all this money."

"We can't," said Ginger. "We've tried."

"We've not *done* anythin'," said William. "Listenin' to a person talkin' isn't *doin'* anythin'. Well, stands to reason you can't cure mental troubles that way. Robert mus' have been muddlin' it up with somethin' else. Member of Parliament or somethin'. Anyway, I'm goin' to be a diff'rent sort of—whatever the word is. I'm goin' to get people out of mental trouble by *doin'* things for 'em. Gosh! Ten shillings!"

"Well, what can you do?" said Ginger. "You can't stop him bein' bored!"

"I bet I can," said William.

"How?"

"Well, I could change the things he's bored with an'

make 'em diff'rent so's he wouldn't be bored with them. He was bored with a holly bush an' white paint an' chair covers. I bet I could change them easy."

"You don't even know where he lives."

"I could find out," said William. "He said he lived in Green Lane an' there was a holly bush in the garden. We could go an' have a look. I'm gettin' sick of listenin' to people talkin'. Gosh! I've had enough of listenin' to people talkin' to last me the rest of my life."

"What about the other man?" said Ginger.

"I'm not goin' to bother about *him*," said William. "It was a soppy mental trouble, anyway, an' he only gave us threepence. But—ten *shillings*! . . . Come on. Let's go an' find Green Lane."

They took the notice from the barn door and made their way across the fields to Marleigh.

Green Lane was a pleasant, secluded little lane with a few detached houses standing well back from the road. Only one had a holly bush in the garden. William and Ginger stood looking at it."

"That's the one," said William. "Now we've got to think what to do."

"We could cut down the holly bush," said Ginger. "He said it got on his nerves."

"No, we'd better not go messin' about with trees," said William. "I got into an awful row once for graftin' an apple tree of my father's on to one of his rhododendrons. You'd have thought he'd have *liked* to have apples on his rhododendrons, but he made an awful fuss. We'd better leave trees alone."

"What can we do, then?" said Ginger.

"There's the chair covers," said William, frowning thoughtfully, "but we can't do much about chair covers. There's the white paint an'——" The frown cleared from his face. It shone with the dawning of an idea. "Gosh! I *know* what we'll do. He said the white paint got on his nerves an' there wasn't any colour in his life. Well, we'll *put* some colour in it. We'll put some colour on the white paint. There's half a tin of red paint in our garage an' about quarter of a tin of yellow. Is there any in yours?"

"Yes," said Ginger. "My mother was paintin' the kitchen cupboard blue an' there's about half a tin of it left. An' there's some of the green left that my father was paintin' the gate with."

"Gosh!" said William. "Green an' blue an' yellow an' red! We can put some colour in his life now all right, an' stop that white paint gettin' on his nerves."

"My mother's goin' out to tea," said Ginger, "an' I can't get the tins

ON BOTH THEIR FACES WAS AN
EXPRESSION OF STERN PURPOSE.

till she's gone. She'd make an awful fuss if she saw me gettin' them, an' she'd be sure to if she was at home."

"All right," said William. "You come along for me as soon as she's gone an' we won't get the helicopter till we've done it. We'll have it done by the time he comes home. It'll be a nice surprise for him."

Later in the afternoon the two set out across the fields, carrying a tin of paint in each hand. On both their faces was an expression of stern purpose. Again they halted at the gate of the house with the holly bush in the garden.

"There might be someone in," said Ginger.

"Gosh! I never thought of that," said William. "I'll go an' find out. I'll pretend I've come to see the gas meter."

"They'll know you couldn't have," said Ginger.

"All right, I'll pretend I'm trying to sell washin' machines."

"They'd know you couldn't be doin' that, too," said Ginger.

"All right," said William a little flatly, accepting the limitations of reality. "I'll jus' ask the time."

He went to the front door and beat a loud tatttoo with the knocker. No one appeared. He repeated the performance. Still no one appeared. He turned to Ginger and beckoned.

"Let's go round to the back," he said.

They went round to the back. Again William knocked at the door. Again no one appeared. He tried the door. It was locked. He surveyed the structure of the house. A garden seat, which stood against the kitchen wall, gave easy access to a sloping roof, which,

in its turn, gave easy access to a window open at the
bottom.

"Come on," said William, beginning to mount the
seat. "I thought there'd be a bathroom window you
could get into. There gen'rally is. I'm jolly good at
bathroom windows. I always get into ours when my
mother's forgot her key." Encumbered by their pots
of paint, the two made a slow and laborious ascent but
at last found themselves in a small, neat bathroom,
with a neat row of toilet appliances on a shelf and a
neat row of towels on a rail.

"Come on downstairs," said William. "It's the
downstairs he doesn't like."

They went downstairs and entered a small, neat
sitting-room with white-painted mantelpiece, white-
painted door, white-painted skirting-board, parchment-
coloured walls and cretonne-covered chairs.

"Let's start on the mantelpiece," said William.
"We'll have it red, shall we?"

"No, yellow," said Ginger.

"Red *an'* yellow," said William.

"Yes, an' a bit of blue."

"All right. An' we might as well put a bit of green
on, too."

They opened the tins of paint. William took his
brushes from his pocket.

"Come on," he said, a note of joyful anticipation in
his voice. "Let's start sloshin' it on. You start sloshin'
red from one side an' I'll start sloshin' blue from the
other an' we'll go on till we meet an' then we'll fill up
the bits we've left with the yellow an' green."

They put the four paint pots on the hearth and set
to work. Red, blue, green and yellow spread over the

mantelpiece and its surround in great uneven sweeps, fell in blobs on to the hearth, crept into William's hair, over Ginger's pullover and legs.

Finally they stepped back and surveyed the result with critical frowns.

"Looks jolly fine to me," said William.

"Does to me, too," said Ginger. "It ought to cheer him up all right."

"Now we'll do that bit round the bottom of the walls," said William. "We'll do it in patches same as the mantelpiece. I think patches look jolly nice."

They did it in patches—red, blue, green and yellow. The paint spread up William's arms, down Ginger's neck, over both their faces. Again they stepped back to consider the result.

"Well, I mus' say I like it," said William. "Don't you?"

"Yes, I do," said Ginger. "It jus' couldn't *help* cheerin' anyone up."

"We've still got the door to do," said William, "an' there's not much paint left. I don't think we'll try paintin' it all over. We'll jus' do a few big sloshes . . ."

They did a few big sloshes—bold thrusts of paint that seemed to leap hilariously across the white surface.

William looked round him. The urge to paint was mounting to fever pitch.

"It makes the wall look jolly dull," he said. "Let's slosh a bit on the walls. There's some yellow an' red left. I'm goin' to slosh the yellow on first."

He executed a few large sweeps of yellow on the wall and was just taking up the tin of red paint when Ginger, who was standing by the window, spoke in a tense whisper.

"He's comin', William. He's comin' down the road."

"Who?" said William.

"The man that lives here. The man you did this mornin'."

"Good!" said William. "I'll go'n' meet him."

He was at the gate when Mr. Summers reached it.

"Come on in," said William urgently. "We've got somethin' to show you."

Looking a little mystified, Mr. Summers followed him up the path, into the house, into the sitting-room.

"Well, what do you think of it?" said William, waving a hand round the scene.

"It's—colourful," said Mr. Summers.

"Do you like it?" said William.

"It would take some getting used to," said Mr. Summers.

"Well, you'll soon get used to it," said William, "an' anyway, it isn't dull."

"Oh, no," agreed Mr. Summers, "and presumably whoever lives here must like this sort of thing."

"But it's your house, isn't it?" said William.

"No, it's not my house," said Mr. Summers.

William's mouth dropped open.

"But you live here."

"No, I don't."

"B-but you said there was a holly bush in your garden."

"The holly bush is in my back garden," said Mr. Summers. "My house is at the farther end of the lane."

"Gosh!" said William, looking round at his handiwork in mounting apprehension. "I wonder who does live here."

WILLIAM'S MOUTH DROPPED OPEN.
"BUT YOU LIVE HERE." "NO, I
DON'T."

"I've no idea," said Mr. Summers. "I'm afraid I
haven't made contact with any of my neighbours."

"Gosh!" said William again faintly.

They heard the click of the front gate and looked out
of the window.

Mr. Peaslake was entering what was obviously his
own domain.

They stood there, silent, motionless, listening to the

sound of footsteps passing through the hall . . . and out into the back garden.

"Come on!" whispered William. "Out of the front! Quick!"

They went into the hall and opened the front door. A car was just drawing up at the gate, a woman at the steering wheel. She had a thin, earnest-looking face, framed in loops of auburn hair. She wore a sack-like dress, smocked at neck and waist. Necklaces of brightly coloured beads dangled over her chest.

"Gosh! We can't go out there now," whispered William, closing the door. "Upstairs, quick! We'll get out of the bathroom window."

As if hypnotised, Mr. Summers followed them upstairs. They entered the bathroom and looked cautiously out of the window. The garden seat had gone from beneath the wall. Mr. Peaslake had set it up

beside his rose garden and was now occupied in cutting
off dead blooms from his rose bushes.

"We can't get down without the seat," said William.
He turned to Mr. Summers. "I bet you couldn't, anyway."

"No, I don't think I could," said Mr. Summers.

He wore a trance-like air, as if swept into a situation
so far removed from reality that all he could do was
to accept it blindly.

There came the sound of a knock at the front door,
footsteps crossing the hall and the opening of the front
door.

"Amanda!" cried Mr. Peaslake in a tone of mingled
joy and anguish.

"Will you come and help me with the spin dryer,
Albert?" said a clear resonant voice.

"Yes, dear," said Mr. Peaslake miserably.

They went down towards the car.

"Come on, quick!" said William. "Come on an' out
at the back!"

They had reached the foot of the stairs when there
came again the sound of the clear resonant voice. "Go
and get a receptacle of some sort for the casseroles,
Albert," and they heard hasty footsteps returning to
the house.

"Quick! In here!" said William, opening the door
of a cupboard beneath the stairs.

The three squeezed into it with some difficulty.
William had on several occasions taken refuge in cup-
boards beneath stairs and this was one of the smallest
he had ever known. Moreover, it was already almost
filled by brooms and brushes and other household
equipment. He looked round it with disapproval.

"Hardly room to *breathe*!" he said indignantly.

A small shelf ran over the door. William set his tin of paint carefully on the shelf and applied his ear to the keyhole.

"Can't see anythin'," he whispered, "but listen!"

There was a sound suggestive of some heavy article being moved across the hall . . . then footsteps passing to and fro . . . then Amanda's voice.

"I think those are all the presents, Albert. There wasn't room in the car for the sack of potatoes. I'll send it later by the carrier. It was a kind thought but I seldom eat them. I find that they have a clogging effect on the mental faculties. Well, I'll be going now."

"Just come into the sitting-room and rest for a moment," pleaded Mr. Peaslake.

"Just for a moment," agreed Amanda grudgingly.

There was a short silence, broken by a cry of "Albert!"

A gasp of horrified amazement from Mr. Peaslake was drowned by another cry of "Oh, *Albert*!". Amanda's voice rose in ecstasy. "Oh, Albert, how marvellous! How *too* contemporary! How utterly out of the world of the suburbs. Why, it's *fauve*. Pure *fauve*. How I've misjudged you, Albert! I can see that I've interrupted you in the middle of it and that it needs a little finishing off. But not too much, Albert, I beg. That unfinished look is too perfect. It's the very essence of primitive art. And to think that I found you conventional, that I thought you lacked the vital spark! You have it indeed!"

"You mean—you mean you don't want to break off the engagement?" faltered Mr. Peaslake.

"Oh, no, Albert! Not now I've come to know you

B

as you really are. Not now I've found the vital spark in you. I shall always know it's there now." She gave a playful laugh. "However stodgy you may seem on the surface, I shall always know the *real* Albert now. Let's put the presents back in the car, dear. They will all mean so much to me now. And I'm afraid I must run off. I'm due at a meeting of Sacla."

"S-sacla?" stammered Mr. Peaslake.

"Society for the Abolition of the Conventional in Life and Art, dear. I'm on the committee, you know, and I'm late already . . . I must certainly give them an account of your new scheme of decoration."

There followed the sound of the spin dryer and casseroles and other articles being conveyed back to the car.

Mr. Summers spoke for the first time.

"You wouldn't care to tell me what all this is about, would you?" he said mildly.

"We were tryin' to cure you of mental troubles," said William.

"You said you were bored with your house," said Ginger.

"We wanted to put some colour in your life same as you said."

"'Cause of the helicopter."

"'Cause of the *two* helicopters. We can get two for ten shillings."

"We thought you lived here."

"It was the holly bush sent us wrong."

"We wanted you to have a bit of colour 'stead of the white paint."

"'Cause it was on your nerves."

And suddenly Mr. Summers began to laugh. It was

a faint, rather rusty laugh at first, but it gathered strength as the full force of the situation struck him.

Mr. Peaslake watched the car out of sight then returned to the house.

He stood for a moment in the doorway of the sitting-room, looking round with an expression of blank be-wilderment.

Then he noticed strange sounds coming from the cupboard beneath the stairs. Approaching it slowly and fearfully, he flung open the door with a violent gesture. So violent was the gesture that it threw him off his balance and brought down the tin of paint on to his head. He sat down heavily, the tin perched on his head, rivulets of yellow paint trickling down his face. And, as he looked at him, Mr. Summers's laughter increased in volume till it resounded through the house in mighty gusts—ear-splitting, Homeric. And suddenly Mr. Peaslake began to laugh, too. He didn't know what he was laughing at. It was partly relief and high spirits, caused by Amanda's change of heart, partly sheer infection from Mr. Summers's laughter.

William was losing interest in the situation.

"Come on!" he said to Ginger. "Let's go an' get those helicopters before the shop closes."

They went out of the cupboard, out of the house, down to the gate. Gusts of laughter followed them along the road.

Suddenly and for the first time, Ginger noticed their paint-bespattered appearance.

"I say!" he said. "We're goin' to get into an awful row when we get home."

"Never mind," said William philosophically. "We'll have got the helicopters an' we've cured 'em of mental troubles. We've cured 'em both of mental troubles. Gosh!" His voice rose exultantly, and a swagger invaded his walk. "I mus' be a jolly good—whatever the word is. I've cured *two* in one day. I've cured every single one that's been to me. I bet I'd easy make myself famous at it." A thoughtful frown wrinkled his brow. "But I don't think I'll be one, after all. I don't want to be somethin' I can't remember the name of. I'm goin' back to somethin' that's easier to say. I'm goin' back to bein' a diver."

II

VIOLET ELIZABETH'S PARTY

"SHE'S still comin'," said Ginger, throwing a hasty glance behind him.

"Let's dodge into the wood an' throw her off the scent," suggested Henry.

"We've tried that," said Douglas with a hollow laugh. "It's never been any good yet."

"Let's hide somewhere," said Ginger.

"*That's* never been any good either," said Douglas with another hollow laugh.

"No, she's got as many eyes as an octopus," said William morosely.

"Let's try it, anyway," said Henry. "Come on!"

They dodged into the wood and hastened down the narrow path.

Ginger glanced back. The small resolute figure of Violet Elizabeth could be seen winding its way behind them through the trees.

"She's still comin'," he said.

"Let's run," said Douglas.

"Gosh, I'm not goin' to run away from her," said William with spirit. "I'm not goin' to run away from a kid like that. She'd start thinkin' no end of herself if we ran away from her. She'd think we were *scared* of her."

"Well, we are," said Henry simply.

"An' she'd prob'ly catch us up," said Ginger. "She's a jolly good runner."

"We'll jus' take no notice of her," said William. "We'll jus' carry on as if she wasn't there."

"We've tried that before, too," Douglas reminded him.

"Look round an' see if she's still comin'," said William.

"I'm not thill coming, William," said a small triumphant voice. "I've *come*." And they realised that Violet Elizabeth, taking advantage of the moment when their backs were turned, had sprinted nimbly forward and was now walking beside William.

"I thaw you come out," she continued, "tho I thought I'd come out, too."

"Well, now you've come out you can jolly well go back," said Henry.

"Don't talk to her," said William.

"I thought you'd *like* me to come out with you," said Violet Elizabeth plaintively.

"You knew jolly well we wouldn't," said Douglas.

"If you think," said William sternly, "that four *men* like me an' Ginger an' Henry an' Douglas want a batty kid like you trailin' about after them, you're jolly well mistaken."

"I'm not batty, William," said Violet Elizabeth in a tone of disarming meekness, "and I'm not a kid. I'm thix and three quarterth. I'm *old*."

They walked on in silence for some moments. William's idea of ignoring Violet Elizabeth's presence was excellent in theory but never quite successful in practice. Despite Violet Elizabeth's small stature and tender years, she was not easily ignored.

"I THOUGHT YOU'D *LIKE* ME TO COME OUT WITH YOU," SAID
VIOLET ELIZABETH PLAINTIVELY.

"Let's jus' go on talkin' as if she wasn't there," said
William at last.

Another short silence followed, then: "It's a nice day,
isn't it?" said Ginger on an easy conversational note.

"Yes," agreed Henry, keeping a wary eye on the
intruder. "A jolly nice day."

"Doesn't look as if it was goin' to rain," said Douglas, throwing a sidelong glance at Violet Elizabeth.

"Or thunder," said Ginger.

"Or hail," said Henry.

"Or snow," said Douglas.

"Well, it's the middle of summer, you chump," said William, "so it's not likely to."

"It might," said Douglas.

"You never know with weather," said Henry.

The conversation lapsed into silence.

William, having thought of something to say, cleared his throat importantly, then, having forgotten what he was going to say, gave a short unnatural cough and kicked a stone from one side of the path to the other.

The silence was broken by Violet Elizabeth.

"I'm going to have a party," she said.

"Don't take any notice of her," said William.

"And you're all coming to my party," said Violet Elizabeth in a tone of finality.

"We're jolly well *not*," said William, stung into speech.

"Yeth, you are," said Violet Elizabeth serenely. "My mother'th going to thee your motherth and they'll *make* you come."

"If you think," said William, "that anyone's goin' to make *me* come to a rotten ole party of yours——" He ended the sentence with a scornful "Huh!"

"It'th a thpecial party, William," said Violet Elizabeth.

They walked on in silence.

"Don't you want to know what thort of a thpecial party it ith?" said Violet Elizabeth.

"Don't answer her," said William to the others.

"Don't take any notice of her," adding, after a few moments, "What sort of a special party is it, anyway?"

"It'th a mixthure of a party for me an' a party for Aunt Jo."

"Aunt *what*?"

"Aunt Jo. Her nameth Jothephine. Thee'th Mummy'th godmother and thee'th coming to thpend the day with uth and the day thee'th coming ith my birthday, tho Mummy thought thee'd have a thpecial thort of party. An unuthual thort of party."

William gave a snort.

"It'll be that, all right, if *you're* there," he said.

"What *sort* of an unusual party?" said Ginger.

"An old-fathioned thort of party," said Violet Elizabeth. "Mummy thought that Auntie Jo would like the thort of gameth that they had when thee wath a little girl."

"What sort of games did they have?" said William.

"Gameth like Pothtman'th Knock."

"Gosh! What's that?" said William.

"It'th a nithe game," said Violet Elizabeth. "Thomeone goeth out into the hall and then knockth at the door and thayth 'A letter for thomeone' and the perthon who'th name they thay hath got to go out into the hall and kith them. And if they thay 'two letterth' they've got to give them two kitheth, and if they thay 'three letterth' they've got to give them three kitheth and if they thay 'ten letterth'——"

"Shut *up*!" said William. His face had blanched with horror. "*Gosh!* It you think we're going to a party with sickenin' games like that, we'd—we'd——"

"We'd rather die a thousand deaths," supplied Henry, who had a large range of dramatic expressions.

"Yes, we jolly well would," said William. "*More* than a thousand. I'd rather die *ten* thousand than play a sickening game like that."

"It'th not a thickening game, William," said Violet Elizabeth. "It'th a nithe game. It'th not *rough* like Cowboyth and Indianth. And we're going to have another old-fathioned game called 'Kith in the Ring'. Mummy sayth it'th a *thweet* game. And you'll have to come to the party, cauthe my mother'th going to thee your motherth and they'll *make* you come."

"Huh!" said William. "I bet our mothers have got a bit more sense than *that*. I bet our mothers'll feel the same as what we do. I bet our mothers would—would rather die a thousand deaths than let us go to a sickening party like that."

But his heart sank when he reached the gate of his home and saw the plump, over-dressed figure of Violet Elizabeth's mother filling, almost to overflowing, the small arm-chair by the window.

He opened the front door silently, inch by inch, tip-toed into the hall and stood for a moment, wondering whether to retreat to the refuge of his bedroom or go into the sitting-room and learn the worst.

He decided to go into the sitting-room and learn the worst.

He opened the sitting-room door and stood there, turning his ferocious scowl from his mother to Mrs. Bott, from Mrs. Bott to his mother.

"Oh, there you are, love," said Mrs. Bott. "I've just been telling your mother about a nice little treat I've got for you."

"I'd rather die a thous——" began William.

"Say 'how d'you do', dear," said Mrs. Brown hastily.

"How d'you do!" said William, intensifying his ferocious scowl and trying to infuse a dark and ominous threat into the words.

Mrs. Bott beamed at him complacently.

"Dear little chap!" she said. "He has his little shy turns same as any other child, after all, hasn't he? . . . Well, Mrs. Brown, as I was telling you, this godmother of mine that I've not seen for years is comin' over to spend the day with us and the day she's chose 'appens to be Vi'let Elizabeth's birthday." Mrs. Bott paused; then, as was her occasional custom, leisurely collected the missing aspirate. "*H*appens. So I thought I'd kill two birds with one stone, as it were, an' sort of make Vi'let Elizabeth's birthday a reel treat for this Aunt Jo of mine. I thought I'd have a children's party but with the old-world games that people used to have at children's parties when she was a child. It'd be a bit out of the ordinary. I mean, it'd be somethin' that's never been done before. I've always"—wistfully—"wanted to do something that's never been done before, but I've never been able to think up anything. It'd be a nice little treat for Aunt Jo an' it'd be great fun for the kiddies."

William uttered a sound that was meant to be a grunt of disgust but that sounded like a low growl.

"Be quiet, dear," said Mrs. Brown.

"It's all them ice-creams he eats," said Mrs. Bott. "They lays 'eavy on the stomach. *H*eavy. Well, about this 'ere children's party. I'm not telling Aunt Jo about it till she comes. It's goin' to be a lovely surprise for her."

"Is she fond of children?" said Mrs. Brown.

Mrs. Bott seemed to consider the question for the first time.

"Well, I suppose so," she said dubiously. "Up to a point. Same as the rest of us, I mean. But"—Mrs. Bott's eyes brightened. Her whole plump little face shone with joy—"I've got hold of a reporter from the *Hadley Times*. Mr. Petersham, the highest-up reporter of 'em all. An' he's going to *do* it. Make a newspaper article out of it. He wouldn't do an ordinary children's party, but he'll do an old-world children's party with sweet old-world games like Postman's Knock and Kiss in the Ring. He's promised me he'll do it. In the paper." A smile of ecstasy again curved Mrs. Bott's lips. "In print."

Mrs. Bott had a secret craving for publicity. She longed to be Somebody. She thirsted to see her name in the paper. Her demands were not exorbitant. A mention in the *Hadley Times* represented the height of her ambition at present, but so far that paper had ignored her activities.

"Not a mention of me winning that there raffle at the Church Fête," she said gloomily, "nor of me gettin' the consolation prize at the W.I. Iced Cake Competition, though I wrote an' told 'im about it special. But he's promised to do this. He says it's News. 'An Original Children's Party' he's goin' to call it an' he's goin' to put it on the front page. So I'm gettin' busy givin' out the invites now to make sure everyone'll turn up. William'll come, of course?"

"Yes, of course he will," said Mrs. Brown, carefully avoiding her son's eye. "Thank you very much, Mrs. Bott."

"Me?" said William in a strangled voice. "*Me?* I'd rather——"

"Of course you'll go, dear," said Mrs. Brown hastily. "It's very kind of Mrs. Bott to ask you."

William glared helplessly.

"You wouldn't think 'e was shy to see 'im about," said Mrs. Bott, "but he'll soon get over 'is shyness once 'e starts rompin' about at them sweet old-fashioned kissin' games."

Mrs. Brown saw her visitor off at the front door and returned, rather apprehensively, to William.

William's face was set in lines of fury and resolution.

"I'm not goin'," he said.

"Don't be silly, dear," said Mrs. Brown. "You'll have to go."

"I'd rather die a thousand deaths," said William.

"Don't be ridiculous, William. One has to be neighbourly. When you're invited anywhere you're expected to go unless you have some good excuse."

"All right," said William. "I've got a good excuse. I've got toothache. I've got to go to the dentist that day."

"If you've got toothache you'd better go to the dentist tomorrow."

"I don't want to go tomorrow. I want to go on the day of the party. Besides, I'm ill. I'm sickenin' for something. If I went to that party I'd give 'em all what I'm sickenin' for an'"—virtuously—"I don't think I ought to. I don't think it'd be *right*."

"If you're feeling ill, dear," said Mrs. Brown, "I'd better ring up the doctor."

"I don't want any ole doctor," said William. "I can tell when I'm sickenin' for somethin' better than any ole doctor. Gosh! It's me that's sickenin', isn't it, not *him*. . . . Besides, I've got an important engagement that day. I can't poss'bly go."

"What important engagement?" challenged Mrs. Brown.

"It's somethin' secret I can't talk about," said William. "It's somethin'—somethin' that the fate of nations depends on." The thrilling imaginary existence that William led as a Secret Service spy became suddenly more real than the actual world around him. "Gosh! I can't *talk* about it. Gosh! There's people's lives hangin' on threads by it. There's—there's webs of myst'ry an'—an' tangled lab'rinths of crime an'—an' people walkin' on razors' edges an'——"

"Now, William, you're just talking nonsense," said Mrs. Brown calmly. "You've not given me one single sensible reason why you can't go."

"Yes, I have," said William.

"What is it?"

"That I'd rather die a thousand deaths," said William.

"Don't be foolish, William," said Mrs. Brown. "In a small place like this, you know, one can't afford to offend people. Mrs. Bott isn't an easy woman. She goes up in the air about nothing at all. She'll be sure to take offence if you don't go and I—well, I just can't be bothered by it."

"An' what about me?" burst out William. "What about me suffering untold ag'ny in those awful games?"

"Oh, it won't be as bad as all that, William," smiled Mrs. Brown. "It'll soon be over. Only an hour or two and then you can forget all about it."

"Can I?" said William darkly. "I've heard of people that had their hair turned white by a few hours of untold ag'ny. Well, don't blame me if I come back from that ole party with my hair white." He gave his short ironic laugh. "I'll look jolly funny, won't I, goin' about for the rest of my life with my hair white, an' all because you made me go an' suffer untold ag'ny at that batty party."

"It's no use talking about it," said Mrs. Brown. "You'll have to go and that's all there is to it."

A meeting with Ginger, Henry and Douglas the next day did little to raise William's spirits. Each of their mothers had adopted the same attitude as Mrs. Brown.

"More like—like—like *hyenas* than yuman parents," said Ginger bitterly.

"Yes, look at me!" said William. "*Torchered* by toothache, sickenin' for an *awful* disease an' with the fate of nations hangin' on me by threads an' I've got to go to a batty kids' party. She doesn't seem to care about my hair turnin' white. Gosh! I bet even a *hyena*'d care about its son's hair turnin' white."

"I told mine I didn't think I ought to go to a party," said Henry. "My aunt was saying the other day that it was this mad pursuit of pleasure that was the curse of the age an' turned people into hooligans so I said I'd start givin' up this mad pursuit of pleasure by not goin' to Violet Elizabeth's party. You'd've thought they'd have been pleased, but they weren't. Well, it'll be their own fault if I turn into a hooligan an' a curse of the age, same as what she said."

"I told mine I thought I ought to be *studyin'* instead of wastin' my time at parties," said Ginger. "I said I was backward in nat'ral hist'ry an' I ought to go into the woods an' study it."

"That was a good idea," said William with a touch of envy in his voice. He hadn't thought of that one.

"It wasn't any good," said Ginger gloomily. "They

keep sayin' I ought to take my school work more seri-
ously an' then when I try to they send me off to batty
kids' parties."

"I told them I'd rather die a thousand deaths," said
William.

"So did I," said Ginger, Henry and Douglas.

"Gosh!" said William helplessly. "You wouldn't
b'lieve it, would you? Four yuman parents lettin' their
sons die a thousand deaths jus' to stop one dotty ole
woman goin' up in the air!"

"We can't get out of it, I s'pose," said Douglas with
a sigh. "We'll have to wash our faces an' necks an'
ears and brush our hair an'"—his mind dwelt with
morbid relish on the scene—"put on clean shirts an'
best suits an' tight garters an' they'll stand at the
window to make sure we go off to it."

"Y-yes," said William thoughtfully, "but they can't
do more than that."

"What d'you mean?"

"They won't *take* us there. They don't *take* us to
parties now. They only took us to parties when we
were young. They've not taken us to parties for years."

"Well, how's that goin' to help?" said Ginger.

"We can start out to it," said William. "But"—his
voice sank to a sinister note—"we needn't ever get
there."

"Gosh!" said Douglas apprehensively. "What's
goin' to happen to us?"

"We'll meet," said William. "We'll meet at the
cross-roads near the Hall an' we'll go off to the woods.
We won't *go* to the ole party. I once heard someone say
that it was the *juty* of every one to fight against tyranny
an' this sickenin' party's tyranny, so that's what

we'll do. We'll go an' do our juty fightin' against tyranny."

They considered the suggestion for a moment or two in silence with mingled excitement and misgiving.

"We'll die a thousand deaths all right when they find out," said Ginger.

"Very well," said William. "If you'd rather play sick'nin' games with Violet Elizabeth Bott an' her sick'nin' ole aunt, you can. I'm goin' off to the woods an' if you don't want to come with me, don't."

But they did want to come with him. They clamoured to come with him. They flung their doubts aside and viewed the prospect with spirits that rose higher the more they viewed it.

"We'll have a jolly good time," said William. "It doesn't matter what we do 'cause we'll be gettin' in a row anyhow so we might as well get in a big one as a little one."

"A big one's more excitin' than a little one, in a way," said Henry.

"Makes it more worth while," said Ginger.

"Well, this ole party starts at half past three," said William. "So we'll meet at the cross-roads jus' before then an' we'll go off to the woods an' have a jolly good time."

Mrs. Brown was surprised by William's meekness and docility when the time came to prepare him for the party. She had expected passionate protests, wild excuses, torrential spates of eloquence, but it was in (comparative) silence that he allowed himself to be cleaned, scoured, brushed and encased in his best clothes, like an offering decked for sacrifice.

Mrs. Brown was touched and even a little remorseful.
"I'm sure you'll enjoy it, dear," she said.
"Yes, I bet I will," said William.
"You'll be glad you went."
William agreed.
"And perhaps your father and I will give you a little
something this evening in return for whatever you've
been through."
William thought that, too, highly probable.
Shining with cleanliness, their shoes brightly polished,
their stockings neatly gartered, the Outlaws assembled
at the cross-roads. They looked at each other sheep-
ishly, awed by the immensity of the crime they
were about to commit. Never before had they—or,
indeed, any of their acquaintances—played truant from
a party.
"Well, come on," said William gruffly. "Let's get
away quick before anyone sees us."
They set off down the road and entered the woods,
walking in a furtive guilty fashion down the shady path.
They felt ill at ease in their best suits and polished shoes.
They felt vaguely ashamed to be there, brushed and
cleaned and neatly apparelled, in a place that was
wont to see them muddy and dishevelled, wearing battle-
scarred shorts and pullovers.
"I wonder what they'll do when they find we're not
comin' to it," said William.
"They'll ring up our mothers," said Ginger.
"An' then they'll ring up the p'lice," said Henry.
"Gosh!" said Douglas, with mingled apprehension
and pride. "Real p'licemen lookin' for us!"
"An' all our mothers wonderin' where we are!" said
Ginger.

"I bet mine'll guess all right," said William gloomily.

"Could we pretend we'd tried a short cut through the woods an' got lost?" suggested Ginger.

"No," said William. "You can't get lost in a place that you've lived in all your life."

"We might pretend we'd lost our memories," said Henry.

"I've tried that," said William. "It didn't work."

"We could pretend we'd met a hypnotiser an' got hypnotised," said Ginger after a moment's silence. "We could act as if we'd been hypnotised. We could keep shuttin' our eyes an then openin' them an' sayin' 'Where am I?'"

"Or that we'd heard cries for help an' gone to the rescue."

"Or that we'd been dragged into the woods by smash-an'-grab thieves an' tied to a tree an' robbed."

"Or that we'd gone to save an old man's life that was bein' attacked by—by a savage animal. A fox, f'rinstance."

"Foxes aren't savage animals."

"This one might have been. It might have gone mad."

"Or the old man might have gone mad."

"Or they might both have gone mad an' turned on us, both ravin' mad."

"An' chased us round the woods . . ."

"So's we had to climb a tree to escape the jaws of death . . ."

"An' then, jus' when we thought we'd escaped them, they climbed it, too, both ravin' mad . . ."

"An' we had to swing ourselves into the nex' tree by the branches . . ."

"Foxes can't climb trees."

"I bet a mad one could."

"An' we had to keep swingin' ourselves from tree to tree with this mad old man an' this mad fox after us . . ."

"Roarin' an' growlin'——"

"Snappin' at our heels——"

"With the jaws of death loomin' in front of us."

They found the imaginary adventure exhilarating and might have continued it indefinitely if Douglas had not distracted their attention by making a sudden dive behind a bush.

"What's the matter?" said William.

"Nothin'," said Douglas, emerging with a nervous apologetic smile. "I thought for a minute that I heard that p'liceman comin' after us." He looked up and down the empty path. "But I couldn't have."

"'Course you couldn't, you chump!" said William. "Gosh! Fancy bein' afraid of a p'liceman, anyway. They're only yuman, same as everyone else. Why, I once met one that kept a goldfish."

But something of Douglas's nervousness had communicated itself to them.

"P'raps we'd better get off the path for a bit," said William, "jus' in case someone comes after us."

He led the way off the path to a fallen log at the foot of an oak tree, screened from the path by a dense holly bush. They had used the log frequently as a jumping-off ground to the lowest branch of the oak tree, but, though they looked up at it longingly, they lacked the spirit to add to the dark crime of playing truant from a party the further and darker crime of climbing trees in their best clothes. They took their seats in a row on the log—four immaculately clothed, somewhat worried-looking small boys.

"I bet mine won't let me go to the fair next week after this," said Ginger gloomily.

"I don't s'pose mine'll give me any pocket-money for the rest of my life," said Henry.

"An' I bet, if this p'liceman catches us, he'll drag us off to prison," said Douglas. "I don't see how keepin' a goldfish is goin' to stop him."

"We'll all die a thousand deaths one way or another," said Henry.

"An' it'll be *worth* it," said William with spirit. "Gosh! I'd *enjoy* dyin' a thousand deaths to get out of that soppy party."

"Yes, we would, too," they assured him, taking courage, as usual, from his buoyant confidence. "'*Course* we would."

"D'you know what I think?" said Ginger slowly. "I think it's civ'lisation that's wrong. If there wasn't any civ'lisation, there wouldn't be any soppy parties. Someone ought to put a stop to it."

"Yes," agreed Henry. "I can't think why people've gone on with it all these years. I heard someone talkin' about a book they'd read the other day an' it was about some people that were all there was left after an atom war an' they were startin' civ'lisation again, but they wanted a *better* civ'lisation."

"That was a jolly good idea," said William. "Gosh! Wouldn't it be fun if jus' us four were left after an atom war an' we could start a better civ'lisation?"

"Yes," said Henry. "These people wanted to start a civ'lisation that was all art an' learnin' an' no war."

"Dunno about that," said William doubtfully.

"We've tried learnin' an' there's not much sense in it. Gosh! We've wasted years of our life wearin' out our brains over arithmetic an' hist'ry an' stuff an'—well, there jus' isn't any *sense* in it. I think civ'lisation'd be better without learnin'."

"There's not much sense in art, either," said Ginger.

"No, there isn't," agreed William. "What's the

"WHAT ARE YOU DOING HERE?" SAID THE NEWCOMER.

point of *drawin'* things? It's a batty thing to do. There's trees an' animals an' rivers an' such-like in real life an' they're all right in real life, but what's the point of *drawin'* them on pieces of paper? You can't climb a tree on a piece of paper or ride a horse on a piece of paper or swim a river on a piece of paper, so what's the point of puttin' 'em there? Why not leave 'em in real life where they b'long?"

"An' war . . ." said Henry.

"War's wrong," said Douglas primly.

"It's weapons that's wrong," said William. "War's all right without weapons. You can have a jolly good fight without weapons. We'd keep war but not weapons."

"We could have sticks," said Ginger. "A stick's jolly useful in a fight."

"Yes," agreed William. "When countries went to war we'd have 'em all meetin' in a big empty place an' everyone could have a stick an' they could fight there an' the side that ran away would have lost the war an' the other side would have won it. It needn't take long. I've been in some jolly good fights that were over in a few minutes."

"I've known 'em take longer than that," said Douglas.

"Well, if it was a long one we could have half-time with ice creams . . ."

"An' lollies——"

"An' choc'lates——"

"An' coco-nut ice——"

"An'——"

"Hush!" said Douglas. "There's someone comin'."

They listened. Footsteps were approaching along the woodland path.

"Freeze," whispered William urgently. "Try'n' look like tree-trunks."

Without much success they tried to look like tree-trunks. Douglas's face grew purple with the effort. Henry grabbed a leafy twig and put it in his mouth, swallowing half of it by mistake. Ginger drew the collar of his jacket as far as it would go over his head. William contented himself with fixing a set ferocious glare on the holly bush.

The footsteps drew nearer . . . and suddenly a small upright figure appeared. It was an elderly woman, wearing boots, a pork-pie hat and a large tweed over-coat. She strode along the path, using a long, folded umbrella as a walking-stick. She did not glance in their direction till—just when the danger seemed over—Douglas, relaxing from the tension of being a tree, fell over backwards and let out a loud yell as his head struck the ground. The woman stopped and threw a startled glance around. The startled glance rested on the Outlaws, and she strode up to them through the bushes.

"What are you doing here?" she said.

They looked at her, scowling suspiciously.

"Just sittin'," said William coldly.

"Restin'," said Ginger.

"Thinkin'," said Douglas.

"Havin' a little talk about civ'lisation," said Henry, removing the remains of his twig from his mouth.

"I'll join you," said the newcomer, taking her seat at the end of the log. She had a small wizened face, bright blue eyes and a long humorous mouth. "I'm rather tired. . . . And what do you think about civilisation?"

"I wouldn't have any grown-ups in it if I had *my* way," said William.

He was outraged by this invasion of their privacy. His scowl had grown so ferocious that every feature in his face seemed to be distorted by it. This woman, he thought, might betray their hiding-place. She must be got rid of as soon as possible. He added his petrifying glare to his ferocious scowl. The woman seemed un-moved by it.

"And I wouldn't have any children," she said. She gave a sudden chuckle. "You'll never guess what I'm doing now."

William was silent for a moment or two, torn between his natural curiosity and his desire to freeze off the intruder by ignoring her. His natural curiosity won.

"What?" he said.

"I'm running away from a children's party."

They stared at her.

"Oh," said William blankly.

"Yes, I'll tell you about it. It's rather a long story. I don't know whether you know a ghastly child who lives in the neighbourhood called Violet Elizabeth Bott. . . ."

"Well, yes," said William guardedly. "In a sort of a way we do."

"We've *heard* of her," said Henry, imitating William's caution.

"I think we've seen her," said Ginger.

"Once or twice," said Douglas.

"I b'lieve she lives somewhere near here, doesn't she?" said William, assuming the imbecile expression that he fondly imagined to denote wondering innocence.

"Oh, yes. Quite near. At the Hall," said the woman. "Well, I'm her mother's godmother and that's how the whole thing begins. Aunt Jo, she calls me. I couldn't stand her even as a child. I haven't seen her for donkey's years. She's been pestering me to come and see her and I've kept putting it off, but I happened to be passing through this part of the country, so I thought I'd take the bull by the horns and get it over.

So I wrote and told her that I'd spend today with them. Actually I'm on my way to Paris. I go to Paris once a year to get the cobwebs blown away. I arrived this afternoon and I find that it's the revolting child's birthday and they're having a party for it—and for me, I gather. A children's party, if you please. And, to add the final touch of horror, they're going to have those nauseating kissing games that made children's parties torture to me when I was a child.

"Well, I told myself that I was her guest and must just go through with it—*noblesse oblige* and 'theirs not to reason why' and the rest of it—and then I suddenly realised that I couldn't. The very thought of it turned my stomach and chilled my blood. I remembered that once when I was a child I'd run away from a children's party and I decided to do it again. So I just sloped off and here I am!"

William drew a deep breath.

"Gosh!" he said faintly.

"If you knew what that child was like, you wouldn't be surprised," said Aunt Jo.

"We do," said William.

"We aren't," said Ginger.

"We'd rather die a thousand deaths," said Henry.

"We sloped off, too, an' here we are, too," said Douglas.

"You mean——"

"We've run away from it, too," said William. "It chilled our stomachs, too."

Aunt Jo's hearty laugh rang out.

"So we're all in the same boat!" she said. "Well, we must stick together. They'll probably send out a search-party." She threw a swift glance round. "You haven't chosen a very good hiding-place. I saw you from the path quite clearly."

"We hadn't got to havin' a hidin'-place yet," said William with dignity. "We were jus' havin' a little talk about civ'lisation. We froze all right. You wouldn't have seen us if Douglas hadn't started yellin'."

"I'm not so sure about that. Anyway, we must find a better one and——"

She stopped abruptly.

There was the sound of voices in the distance. Mrs. Bott's high-pitched voice rent the air.

"Auntie Jo! Auntie Jo!"

Then came a confused murmur of children's voices.

"Heavens alive!" said Aunt Jo. "They're after us! Behind the log, quick!"

Nimbly she flung herself full length behind the log. The others followed. Craning his neck round the edge of the log, William watched a rabble of children, headed by Mrs. Bott, straggle along the path. Violet Elizabeth, looking sulky and aggrieved, brought up the rear.

"We can't start the party without her, that's flat," Mrs. Bott was saying, "an' someone said they'd seen her come into the woods, so in the woods she must be. She must 'ave gone for a little stroll an' lost her way."

"Want to play Pothman'th Knock," shrilled Violet Elizabeth.

"All right, love. You shall. But we've got to find Auntie Jo first. We can't start the party without 'er. She might 'ave tripped over somethin' an' broke her leg. Or got caught up in a rabbit trap. She's close on sixty, poor old dear! She'd be 'elpless in a rabbit trap. Helpless."

"Want to play Pothman'th Knock," wailed Violet Elizabeth.

The little procession straggled on.

Aunt Jo popped up from behind the log.

"The impertinence of the woman!" she said. "'Close on sixty' indeed! I'm sixty-*nine*. Seventy next month. The impertinence! And rabbit trap, indeed! I'd make short work of any rabbit trap, I can tell you. Now come on! We'll get out of the woods and go somewhere else. Follow me!"

She strode on ahead of them, flourishing her umbrella.

William felt slightly disconcerted at having the leadership taken out of his hands. But there was something exhilarating about Aunt Jo, and indeed about the whole situation. All feelings of guilt and apprehension dropped from the four of them as they followed the small resolute figure.

"Once we get out of the woods we'll be all right," said Aunt Jo. "They'll never have the sense to start looking anywhere else. Set of blithering nit-wits!"

But it wasn't so easy to get out of the woods. The search-party had split up and small boys and girls, singly or in couples, were searching the woods. Violet Elizabeth's wail, "Want to play Pothman'th Knock" seemed to rise up from all points of the compass at once. Over and over again Aunt Jo and the four Outlaws had to plunge into bushes or merge themselves hastily into the undergrowth just in time to escape detection. Aunt Jo's spirits seemed to rise higher at each narrow escape.

"Come on!" she would say as she rallied her band, striding on before them, brandishing her umbrella. "Once more into the breach!"

Suddenly William stopped at the end of a path that led under thick, overhanging trees.

"This leads out of the woods," he said. "It's always boggy—dunno why—'specially when it's been rainin', an' it was rainin' last night. Your feet go squishing right into the mud, but I bet you don't mind a bit of mud."

"Indeed I don't," said Aunt Jo. "'Forward the Light Brigade!'"

The path led out of the woods onto the road by the side of a house. Aunt Jo and the four scraped through the hedge that bordered the woods and stopped for a moment by the gate of the house. A large notice "To Let" hung on it.

"Listen!" said Aunt Jo.

The clamour of voices was growing nearer, the voices upraised excitedly. Their pursuers had found their footmarks and were hot on their trail. Aunt Jo threw a glance up and down the road. It held no possible place of concealment.

"Quick! Into the garden!" she said, opening the gate.

The Outlaws followed her into the garden and looked round. It was a square bare patch, enclosed by a fence, without tree or shrub.

"Caught like rats in a trap!" groaned Aunt Jo.

"With our days numbered an' our dooms sealed," said Henry.

But at that moment the door of the house opened and a woman came out, holding a key in her hand.

"Oh, good!" she said. "What a piece of luck! You've come to look over the house, haven't you? Well, I'll give you the key." She handed the key to

Aunt Jo. "Perhaps you'll kindly take it back to the house agent's when you've finished. I promised to take it but I'm catching a train and I'll miss it if I don't make a dash for the bus now." She ran down to the gate. "It's a rotten house," she called as she vanished from sight, "but you may as well look over it now you've come."

"Quick!" said Aunt Jo.

They scrambled into the house and slammed the door.

"Saved!" said Aunt Jo. "Saved by a hairbreadth!"

"From the jaws of a thousand deaths," said William. "They'll get to the end of the path an' they'll not find us an' so they'll go home an' have their rotten old party without us." He looked round at the empty, dust-laden hall and bare uncarpeted staircase. "Gosh! We can have some jolly good games here. Better than any ole Postman's Knock." He went into the back room and called, "This is a *smashing* room. It's got a cupboard all up one side an' a great big fireplace that you can see the sky through the chimney an'—— Gosh! A rat's jus' run off into a hole. We could have a rat hunt here. Let's have a look at the other rooms." He went into the front room and returned almost immediately, looking pale and horror-stricken.

"They're comin'," he said. "They're comin' in through the gate, all of 'em. . . . Gosh! They'll look through the windows an' see us."

"Upstairs, quick!" said Aunt Jo. "Out of their range of vision. Come along. 'On, Stanley, on! Charge, Chester, charge!'"

They plunged upstairs to a landing, up another flight of stairs to another landing, up a narrow ladder set against an open trap-door, into a low-ceilinged attic, with a small dormer window, overlooking the front garden. The attic had evidently been used for storing purposes; rows of apples in various stages of decay lay on slatted shelves along the wall.

William peered through the window.

"Gosh! They're all there," he whispered. "Ole Mr. Bott's with 'em now. They're talkin' away like mad. Let's open the window an' listen."

Cautiously he opened the window and, standing well away from it, they watched the scene below. Violet Elizabeth's party now filled the small front garden. Its members wandered from window to window, looking into the empty rooms. Frankie Parsons was trying ineffectually to climb a piece of trellis. Caroline Jones was pricking blisters of paint with her thumb-nail on one of the window-frames.

Mr. Bott, tired of waiting for them at home, had tracked them down to the empty house, and Mrs. Bott was explaining the situation to him.

"She's been set on by four great men, Botty," she was saying tearfully, "an' dragged into this house."

"How d'you know she has?" said Mr. Bott.

"We found the footmarks along that muddy path. 'Er footmarks an' the footmarks of the four great men that were draggin' her along."

Mr. Bott considered this for a moment or two in silence. Then:

"How d'you know they were her footmarks?"

"'Er boots, Botty. She has 'em made special. With pointed toes. She used to wear 'em like that when she was a girl an' she still has 'em made that way. An' we saw the marks of 'em plain as plain together with the marks of them four great men that were draggin' of her away into this house."

"How d'you know they dragged her into this house?" said Mr. Bott.

"You can see their muddy footmarks on the concrete path goin' up to the front door. Look at 'em, Botty. There's her boots with the pointed toes an' there's the footmarks of them four great men draggin' her along."

"Want to play Pothman'th Knock," demanded Violet Elizabeth shrilly.

"They'll have made away with her by now, like as not," wailed Mrs. Bott. "Oh, Botty, go an' fetch the p'lice quick!"

"Sounds a funny tale to me," said Mr. Bott.

"I want my tea," said Frankie Parsons dolefully.

"I want my tea," chorused the other guests.

"Violet Elizabeth said there was jelly an' sandwiches an' fruit salad," said Frankie Parsons. "I want jelly and sandwiches and fruit salad."

"Want jelly and sandwiches and fruit salad," wailed the chorus.

"Break a window, Botty."

"Them little diamond panes isn't easy to break an' you can't do much when you've broke 'em," said Mr. Bott. "I dunno what to make of it all. I jus' don't."

"And she said there was birthday cake," said Frankie Parsons. "I want some birthday cake."

"Want some birthday cake," clamoured the chorus.

"Oh, Botty, *do* something," said Mrs. Bott hysterically. "They mayn't have finished doin' away with her yet. There may be time to stop 'em. I can't go down to me grave with Auntie Jo's death on me 'ands. *H*ands. A poor helpless old woman like that!"

c

AUNT JO AND THE OUTLAWS HUNG OUT OF THE WINDOW,
HURLING APPLES AT THE CROWD BELOW.

Aunt Jo had been listening with mild amusement,
but at the words "poor helpless old woman" the smile
dropped from her face.

"'Poor helpless old woman'," she echoed indignantly.
"I'll show her!"

She seized one of the rotten apples and flung it with
unerring aim out of the window. It burst with a plop!
full in Mrs. Bott's face.

"Help!" screamed Mrs. Bott. "They've started on
me now. Them murderers 'ave started on *me* now. *Do*
something, Botty."

"Come on," said Aunt Jo gleefully. "Let's give 'em
the rest."

She seized another apple and flung it at Mr. Bott.
It burst with a plop! on his bald head and trickled
down his face. He gave a yell that almost drowned his
wife's screams. Abandoning all attempts at concealment, Aunt Jo and the Outlaws hung out of the window,
hurling apples at the crowd below. They squelched on
heads and shoulders, streamed down faces, bespattered
party frocks and suits. The crowd below retaliated as
best they could, hurling back stones and the remains of

apples, which fell harmlessly against the wall of the house.

Suddenly Frankie Parsons' voice rose again in shrill protest above the tumult.

"It's nearly six o'clock," he said. "My mother'll be comin' for me soon an'"—his voice rose to an indignant squeak—"I've not had any tea!"

Aunt Jo withdrew her head from the window.

"The danger's over," she said. "No time for kissing games now. We can safely make our way down."

"Can't we go on a bit longer?" said William wistfully.

"No," said Aunt Jo. "The party was from three-thirty to six. Our object is accomplished, our triumph won."

Reluctantly they followed her down the staircase. She opened the front door and approached the group outside with a pleasant smile.

"Auntie *Jo*!" gasped Mrs. Bott.

"Yes, dear?" said Aunt Jo innocently.

"What *have* you been doin' of?" said Mrs. Bott in a quavering voice.

"Just looking over the house, dear," said Aunt Jo airily. "I've often thought I'd like a little house in the country. I got the key of this one from the house agent"—she took the key from her pocket and waved it carelessly—"and these boys very kindly came along to help me. But it really isn't suitable. It's too large and very inconvenient. I'm afraid that the inspection has taken longer than I thought it would."

"But—but—but them *apples*!" spluttered Mrs. Bott.

Aunt Jo drew her brows into a puzzled frown.

"Apples?" she said. Then the frown cleared and she smiled as at a sudden memory. "Oh, yes, of course.

Apples. . . . We were inspecting the attics and we found them full of rotten apples. The smell was most unpleasant and unhygenic, so we decided to throw them away." She looked at the apple-bespattered group with a glint of mischief in her eyes. "I'm so sorry if some of them happened to hit you. Well, shall we all go back home now?"

She set off, walking briskly, flourishing her umbrella. The Outlaws followed, Then came the rest of the party, clamouring urgently for its tea. Then came Mr. and Mrs. Bott, Mrs. Bott clinging to her husband and swaying in a somewhat tipsy manner as she walked along the path.

"I'm all of a doo-dah, Botty," she moaned. "I dunno whether I'm standin' on me 'ead or me 'eels. *H*ead. Botty, is she mad or am I?"

"There's times," said Mr. Bott sombrely, "when I think everyone's mad. But don't you worry, love. It'll all come right in the end."

"An' me lovely old-world party with me lovely old-world games! All gone down the drain. There won't be nothin' about it in the newspaper now. I'd been buildin' me 'opes on havin' me party in the paper, Botty. *H*opes. I've always wanted to be in the newspaper, an', try as I will, I never seem to bring it off. An' me feet's that bad with all this trapesing about I don't 'ardly know whether I'm comin' or goin'."

"You're comin', love," said Mr. Bott reassuringly. "Lean on me."

"Tell you what, Botty. . . . I've been thinking."

"Yes, love?"

Mrs. Bott's air of pathos had left her. Her face had darkened ominously.

"I shouldn't be surprised if that there William Brown isn't at the bottom of it all. 'E's at the bottom of everything that goes wrong in this 'ere village."

"But your Aunt Jo . . ."

"She's a poor simple old woman, Botty. William Brown could twist 'er round 'is little finger." She set her lips grimly. "But I'll get the truth out of him. See if I don't."

"Well, we'd better hurry, love. The others are out of sight."

Anger lent speed to Mrs. Bott's feet and she walked almost nimbly down the winding woodland path, along the road and in at the gates of the Hall.

Tea had been laid in the dining-room, and the guests had not waited for the arrival of their hostess. They formed a seething mass round the table, eagerly snatching sandwiches, cakes, biscuits, jellies, trifle. William, Ginger, Henry and Douglas had gone into a huddle over a chocolate mould and were eating it from the dish with tablespoons. Violet Elizabeth was leaning over the table, picking the decorations from her cake and stuffing them into her mouth. Frankie Parsons had spread a sausage roll with strawberry jam and was eating it slowly, with an air of relish. Caroline Jones was sitting under the table drinking fruit salad from a large cut-glass bowl. Cascades of fruit and juice fell from either side of her mouth on to her frock and the carpet, but still she was managing to make a fairly adequate meal. Aunt Jo stood in the window recess, surveying the scene with a sardonic smile. A pallid young man with a nervous expression hovered near the door.

Mrs. Bott entered and threw a lowering glance round the room. It rested finally on the pallid young man.

"'Oo are you?" she said brusquely. "An' what are you doin' 'ere?"

"I'm from the *Hadley Times*," said the young man. "Mr. Petersham couldn't come so he asked me to take his place. I've been watching proceedings"—he gave a nervous smile—"from a respectful distance, of course, all afternoon."

Mrs. Bott sat down, her face blank with dismay.

"You mean . . . You saw what happened?" she gasped.

"Yes." He took a sheet of paper from his pocket. "I've written a somewhat hasty description of it. I'll make any alteration you care to suggest, of course. I'll read it to you, shall I?"

He unfolded the sheet of paper and began to read.

"An Original Children's Party. Yesterday was Miss Violet Elizabeth Bott's birthday and the affair was signalised at the Hall by one of the most original children's parties that have ever taken place in the neighbourhood. Mrs. Bott's first idea was to have an old-fashioned children's party with the old-fashioned games beloved of our great-grandparents. But before the momentous day dawned another idea had flashed into the lady's fertile brain. Not for Mrs. Bott—a child at heart and a sportsman if ever there was one—the conventional party confined to house and garden. Mrs. Bott—a woman of large ideas—conceived something on a more adventurous scale. The party was divided into two, and a grand game of hide-and-seek organised in a neighbouring woods. What fun there was as the children tracked each other along the shady paths of the ancient wood, dodging in and out of the undergrowth, hiding behind the trunks of the old weather-beaten trees that must have seen so many generations of children frolicing in their shade!

"But even such a magnificent game can pall and the resourceful Mrs. Bott had another card up her sleeve. The moment she saw the young guests flagging, the scene was changed, and another game—an even greater tribute to Mrs. Bott's fertile brain—was in full swing. The new game took the form of a siege. For this the enterprising lady had borrowed an empty house, belonging, presumably, to a friend. Again the young guests were divided into two parties. One was the besieged, the other the besiegers . . . and the fun raged fast and furious as they hurled (harmless) missiles at each other with peals of childish laughter. Finally the besieged surrendered and the little band—tired but happy—betook itself to the Hall to tea.

"Here again Mrs. Bott showed her unflagging spirit of enterprise and originality. Not for her the stuffy ceremonial party tea, with children ranged orderly at the table in a depressing atmosphere of manners and decorum. Here again the fun raged fast and furious. It was, in the full sense of that oft misused word, a 'tea fight'. They ate what they wanted, how they wanted, where they wanted. Happy, if grubby, little faces beamed with joy as the table was lightened of its load of abundance. For Mrs. Bott had provided refreshments on a lavish scale and her little guests did them ample justice. But all good things come to an end. Parents arrived to collect their offspring and, one by one, the little guests took their departure, carrying in their hearts a radiant memory that will live with them for many a day.

"Congratulations to Mrs. Bott on the most original children's party that this neighbourhood has ever seen."

He raised his eyes from the paper to Mrs. Bott. "Would you care to suggest any alterations?"

Mrs. Bott was beyond speech. She gasped and blinked. She opened and shut her mouth but no words came.

"I've rather anticipated the end of the party, of course," continued the young man, "but"—he glanced at his watch—"I ought to be getting back to the office."

Suddenly Mrs. Bott found her voice. It was hoarse and unsteady, but still a voice.

"D'you mean," she said, "d'you mean all that what you've just read will be in the newspaper?"

"Oh, yes," said the young man. "Tomorrow, probably."

Mrs. Bott's plump, flushed face relaxed into a smile of ecstasy.

"Crikey!" she breathed. "Well, I never! Thank you *ever* so."

"It's been a pleasure," said the young man.

"Well, 'ave a bit of somethin' to eat before you go," said Mrs. Bott.

The young man glanced at the disordered table and food-scattered floor and repressed a shudder.

"No, thank you so much," he said. He threw her his nervous smile. "Well, good-bye."

He slid swiftly from the room and they saw him pass the window as if in hurried flight.

"Well!" said Mrs. Bott blissfully. "*Well!* Well, I *never*. Jus' *think* of it. Jus' think of everyone *readin'* it in the newspaper. . . . D'you know, I never tumbled to what was 'appenin' all that time. *H*appenin'. Hide-an'-seek an' that there siege." She threw a puzzled glance round. "'Oo's idea was it? Was it yours, Auntie Jo?"

"I won't take all the credit," said Aunt Jo modestly. "I'll share it with William."

"Oh, *William*!" said Mrs. Bott fervently. "'*Ow* I've misjudged you in me thoughts! An' all the time you were plannin' this lovely party with sieges an' what not that's goin' to be in the newspaper." She approached him, beaming affectionately. "Well, I can only say, *thank* you, William Brown, for makin' such a go of it all."

William lifted to her a face plastered from brow to chin with a spoonful of chocolate mould that Ginger had just thrown at him. His glassy smile gleamed faintly through the mask.

"It's been a pleasure," he said politely, as he turned to scoop up a spoonful of jelly from a near-by dish and drop it neatly down Ginger's neck.

III

WILLIAM AND THE HOOP-LA STALL

THE "summer season" of the village was at its
height. Fête succeeded fête, sale of work succeeded
sale of work, flower show succeeded flower show . . . Each
Saturday was a battle-field strewn with nerve-racked
openers, stall-holders, treasurers, rummage collectors,
competition organisers, miniature-train runners, pro-
gramme sellers, tea helpers and refreshment providers.
And the number of Saturdays the summer afforded
proved always insufficient for their needs.

Fête clashed with fête, sale of work with sale of work,
flower show with flower show. Conservatives, Liberals,
Labour, Church, Baptists, Scouts, Guides, Old People's
Homes, Young People's Clubs, scrambled to snatch a
Saturday from the fast diminishing pile. Openers
rushed frantically from one stately home to another,
every household was scoured for the last lonely white
elephant, the last infinitesimal shred of rummage.

William took a mild and slightly cynical interest in
all this. Supporters of Causes would occasionally give
him half-crowns to spend at their fêtes and he would
mooch round the stalls, dive into the bran tub, have a few
shots at the miniature rifle range, consume large quan-
tities of ice-cream and candy-floss, and generally manage
to perform a few acrobatic feats on the roundabout before he was indignantly dismissed by its attendant.

On this particular Friday he was even less than

usually interested in the week-end arrangements. He
knew that a Church fête was to be held in the Vicarage
garden and that a Tennis Club fête was to be held in the
meadow adjoining it. He knew that his sister, Ethel,
was organising the Tennis Club fête and that Mrs.
Monks, the vicar's wife, was organising the Church fête.
He knew that Lady Forrester had, much against her
will, been dug out of her cottage in Little Steedham to
open the Tennis Club fête and that Sir Julius Egerton,
the local M.P., had agreed, at great personal inconvenience, to sandwich the opening of the Church fête between two important political engagements . . . but
William had other things to think of than fêtes. He and
Ginger and Henry and Douglas had planned to have a
game of Cowboys and Indians in which the two Indians
were to ambush the two cowboys, and the details
needed a great deal of thinking out.

He was thinking them out now as he walked along the
road, his hands thrust deep into his pockets, his frowning gaze fixed on the ground, his lips pursed into a shrill
untuneful whistle. He and Ginger would be the Indians
and Henry and Douglas the Cowboys. They would
make the ambush behind the clump of bushes that——
He stopped short. He was passing Archie's cottage and
Archie was there, leaning disconsolately over his ramshackle garden gate.

"Hello," said William.

"Hello," muttered Archie.

Archie generally looked vague and harassed, but
today an unusual air of dejection hung over him.
William abandoned his mental organisation of the
Cowboys and Indians game to concentrate his whole
attention on Archie.

"What's the matter?" he said abruptly. "Is some-thin' worryin' you?"

"Well, yes, it is," admitted Archie.

"What?"

Archie sighed and ran his thin hands through his already disordered hair.

"It—it's about tomorrow."

"What about tomorrow?" said William.

"The fête. The Church fête. I mean, the fête for the Church Restoration Fund."

"Yes, I know," said William, "but you needn't go to it if you don't want to. I'm not goin'."

"Yes, but you see, I *have* to," said Archie. "She's roped me in. She's roped me in for the hoop-la."

"Who has?"

"Mrs. Monks."

"Can't you get out of it?" said William.

"No, I can't. I've tried. You know what she is."

"Yes, I jolly well do," said William.

Everyone knew what Mrs. Monks was. Beneath her bland exterior lay a will power and tenacity of purpose that brooked no opposition. Her tactics were simple. She selected her victim, issued her orders and thereafter ignored protests, resistance and even open rebellion.

"Why didn't you jus' say 'no'?" said William.

"I did," said Archie. "I said it politely, but I said it. And the next day she came round and told me to be there by quarter to two, so I said 'no' again. I still said it politely, of course, but not quite as politely as before, but I really thought it had got through to her at last."

"But it hadn't?" said William.

"No, it hadn't. She sent round a suitcase today full of prizes and things with a note telling me what to do and what not to do."

A far-away look had come into William's eyes. He saw himself presiding over a hoop-la stall, organising his customers, doling out his hoops, presenting his prizes.

"But—Gosh, Archie! You'd have a jolly good time at a hoop-la stall."

"No, I wouldn't," said Archie desperately. "I couldn't. I can't. . . . I mean, I couldn't."

"Why not? Why couldn't you?"

"Well, you see"—something of bashfulness invaded the gloom of Archie's expression—"the Tennis Club fête's tomorrow, too, you know, and Ethel's more or less in charge of it and I'd hoped—I mean, I'd wanted to be free for if she needed me. I've offered to help, of course, in any way I could, but she said she didn't need me . . . Still—one never knows. I hoped that perhaps some last-minute crisis might blow up, but"—despair seemed to engulf him again—"now I'm bound hand and foot to a hoop-la stall."

William shook his head compassionately. He couldn't understand what Ethel's many admirers "saw" in her but, though willing to exploit them in every possible way, he pitied as well as despised them.

"Gosh! I'd sooner have a hoop-la stall than Ethel any day," he said.

"You won't *tell* her about the hoop-la stall, will you?" said Archie anxiously.

"Why not? It might make you seem—sort of more important to her."

"No, no, *no*!" said Archie. "She must look on me as

free and ready to come to her help at once if she needs
me. If necessary I could get someone else to take on the
hoop-la stall."

"I might do it for you," said William casually.

Again he saw himself dispensing hoop-la rings, be-
stowing hoop-la prizes, issuing orders, pronouncing
judgements. "Stand back there!" he heard himself say
in loud imperious tones, "One at a time!"

"You!" said Archie, his voice faint with horror. "I
shouldn't dream of such a thing. I wouldn't trust you
with a hoop, much less a hoop-la stall."

"Very well," said William distantly. "I think I'll be
goin' now. It's nearly tea time."

He walked slowly homeward, his brows furrowed, his
lips grimly set. He was rescuing Archie from incredible
dangers—fire, flood, mad bulls, express trains, run-
away cars—always at the risk of his own life, and
Archie was deeply grateful.

"How I've misjudged you, William!" he said. "How
I wish I'd let you take on that hoop-la stall! I hope you
will forgive me."

And William forgave him.

His self-respect restored by a succession of these
scenes, he entered the front door of his home.

Standing before the mirror in the hall, he practised
his potentate's scowl and his villain's leer, working at
each till he was satisfied. Noticing his father's bowler
hat hanging on a hook, he perched it on his head,
drawing his brows together and narrowing his eyes into
an expression of business-like acumen, which he enjoyed
till an unguarded movement brought the hat down over
his ears. Replacing it on its hook, he tried on a hat and
fur necklet of Ethel's, curving his lips into an inane

simper that broke finally into a guffaw of self-approbation. Then, standing on a chair, he put Ethel's hat on the top of the hat-stand, well out of her reach, before he overbalanced and fell with a clatter on to the floor.

"William!" called Mrs. Brown from the sitting-room.

"That boy!" said Ethel wearily.

William entered the sitting-room, where his mother and Ethel were ticking off a list of tea-tent requirements for the fête; then, realising that he was still wearing Ethel's fur necklet, returned to place it on the hat-stand and re-entered the sitting-room.

"What *have* you been doing, William?" said Mrs. Brown.

William assumed the look of blank imbecility with which he was wont to counter that particular question.

"Nothin'," he said. "Why?"

Mrs. Brown shrugged helplessly and turned again to Ethel.

"Well, you've got everything fixed up now, dear, haven't you?"

"Oh, yes," said Ethel. "The only thing that might fall through is the bran tub. Dolly Clavis is doing it, but she's got a foul cold and may have to cry off at the last minute. If she does I'll get Gordon Franklin to do it."

"His mother told me he was going away for the weekend," said Mrs. Brown.

"Oh well, I can always fall back on Archie," said Ethel carelessly. "He's sure to be at a loose end."

William gave a mysterious snort, but William's mysterious snorts were so familiar that they roused neither interest nor curiosity.

"Well, let's hope that Lady Forrester remembers to turn up for it," said Mrs. Brown. "She's so vague that she hardly ever remembers anything."

"Oh, I think she will," said Ethel, "because she's got a little grandchild over from Canada and she wants her to see a typical English country fête because she's told her so much about them."

"Things so seldom turn out to be typical," said Mrs. Brown with a sigh.

"I don't see why this shouldn't," said Ethel. "The only thing I'm worried about is the wretched bran tub. Anyway, Dolly's gone to bed with a bottle of influenza mixture, so it's sure to be all right in the morning."

But it wasn't all right in the morning. During the night Dolly's cold assumed such virulent proportions that it seemed as if the influenza mixture were determined to justify its name.

"I'b sorry but I just card cub, Ethel," she said thickly over the telephone. "Dot a brad tub adyway. If I had to sped the whole afterdood over a brad tub breathing id brad it would settle od by lugs ad kill be. I expect Archie will see to id for you."

And Archie was delighted to see to it. His long thin face beamed with delight but beneath the delight was an undercurrent of anxiety. Ethel noticed the anxiety.

"Of course, if you don't *want* to," she said coldly.

"Of *course* I want to," Archie assured her earnestly. "You *know* I do. It's only that—what I mean is——"

"If you've made other arrangements . . ." said Ethel.

"No, no, *no!*" said Archie wildly. "I shouldn't dream of doing such a thing. I—I—I'm only too *glad* to do it. You know I am. You——"

"Be in the meadow by one forty-five, then," said Ethel. "All you have to do is to run into Hadley for the bran tub this morning . . . Don't look so flustered, Archie. You needn't worry about the bran tub. Everything's arranged."

Archie wasn't worried about the bran tub. He was worried about the hoop-la stall. Then suddenly he remembered Jameson Jameson. Jameson Jameson was energetic and efficient and public-spirited. Organising a hoop-la stall would be child's play to Jameson Jameson.

It was perhaps unfortunate that William was standing by when Archie agreed to supervise the bran tub. For William decided to take the situation in hand. William enjoyed taking situations in hand and Archie had a fatal weakness for allowing situations in which he was involved to be taken in hand by anyone who was willing to take them.

William followed him out into the road.

"What are you goin' to do?" he said. "I mean about the hoop-la."

"Don't *dare* tell Ethel about the hoop-la," spluttered Archie. "She'd get someone else to do the bran tub, if she knew I'd fixed up to do the hoop-la and—and—and——"

The harassed look on his face faded into a dreamy smile. Ethel was superintending the Tennis fête in the meadow. He would be near her all the time. They would discuss bran and prizes, they would count the money, they even might have tea together, for Ethel, among her many other duties, was in charge of the tea tent. Then the smile faded and the harassed look returned.

" I'll see if Jameson can do it," he went on. "I ought to go over and see him about it at once, but if I've got to fetch the bran tub from Hadley. . . ."

"I'll go'n' ask him, shall I?" said William.

Archie threw him a suspicious glance. William's face wore its look of shining innocence. Archie weakened.

"Well," he said, "I might send a note by you. I couldn't trust you with a message. . . . Yes, I'll write a note. You'll take it round at once, won't you?"

And William took it round at once. He walked sedately down the road to the Jameson house. He barely looked to left or right. He resisted the temptations to vault a five-barred gate, to investigate a suspicious movement in the ditch and to climb a tree that seemed to offer its lowest branch temptingly across the hedge. He passed Bertie Franks, one of his bitterest foes, without a flicker of recognition, ignoring the insolent grimace that Bertie flung at him . . . and finally arrived, neat and tidy, his face stiff and tense with effort, on the front door step of the Jamesons' house.

Jameson Jameson was just emerging from it. He tore the note open.

"No, I can't possibly," he said. "Tell him I can't possibly. I'm just off to judge the children's races at the Liberal fête at Mellings. If I get back in time I'll give him a hand, of course, but I don't think there's much hope of it. I haven't time to write. Just tell him that and get out of my way."

He pushed William from the door step and strode down the garden path.

Slowly, thoughtfully, William set off on his homeward journey. His expression was set and earnest. He

had done his best. He recalled his firm rejection of temptation in the shape of gate, ditch and tree. He recalled
his meek acceptance of Bertie Franks' grimace. The
virtue of the whole proceeding amazed him. It was the
sort of virtue that deserved a reward . . . and a reward it
should have. He would take charge of the hoop-la stall
himself. His slow thoughtful progress turned into a
self-important swagger. There was authority and
dignity in the frowning glance he threw around. His
voice was gruff and imperious as he issued his orders,
"Stand back there! One at a time!"

At a bend of the road he met Archie, rolling a tub
along the road in an uncertain and erratic fashion.
Archie raised a flushed face from his labours.

"Oh, there you are," he said. "Is it fixed up all
right about the hoop-la stall?"

"Yes," said William.

It *was* fixed up all right about the hoop-la stall, he
assured himself, though not quite in the way Archie
meant.

"Good!" said Archie, dismissing hoop-la from his
mind and filling it with roseate visions of a bran tub
aglow with the light of Ethel's presence.

Only a spindly hedge separated the bran tub in the
meadow from the hoop-la stall in the Vicarage garden.
William gazed through it suspiciously, slightly disconcerted by the near proximity of Archie. It was clear,
however, that so far, at any rate, Archie had not noticed
him. Archie was engaged in taking little packets from a
cardboard box and plunging them into the bran tub.
Already bran was seeping along his wrists and arms and
burying itself in his beard.

ARCHIE WAS ENGAGED IN TAKING LITTLE PACKETS FROM A
CARDBOARD BOX AND PLUNGING THEM INTO THE BRAN TUB.

There were very few people round the hoop-la stall. Most of the patrons of the fête had congregated at the point of the hedge where the "openings" were being held. It was a little unfortunate that the openers had taken up their positions on either side of the hedge, separated only by a few yards. Their voices rose in a sort of duet. Sir Julius made his points firmly and forcibly. Lady Forrester's voice was less audible. This, perhaps, was just as well, for Lady Forrester had forgotten to prepare her speech and had snatched up, at the last moment, some notes that she had made for an address to the local branch of the League of Animal Friendship.

"The dignity and beauty of our ancient Parish Church . . ."

"That friend of man throughout the ages, the horse . . ."

"The majestic tower nestling among its immemorial elms . . ."

"Even the humble ant, the timid centipede, the plodding earth worm . . ."

"Our noble heritage . . ."

"Our furred and feathered cousins . . ."

The speeches came to an end (the audience had been chattering together so animatedly that no one had noticed any incongruity in them). The openers bowed distantly to each other over the hedge and went their separate ways. Lady Forrester collected her granddaughter, Angelique, who had taken a pair of binoculars from the White Elephant stall and was perched on the lowest branch of a lop-sided hawthorn tree, surveying the scene, and the two set out for a tour of the stalls.

William, accompanied by Ginger, Henry and Douglas, made his way to the hoop-la stall. Wooden rings lay about in neat little piles, otherwise the table was bare. Nothing daunted, however, the young patrons who were flocking to the stall got busy. Launcelot and Geraint, the Thompson twins, started turning somersaults in the middle of the table. Frankie Parsons and Jimmy Barton seized the rings and began to juggle with them. Bobby Dexter and Victor Jameson began to swing on the ropes that were supposed to hold the contestants at a measured distance from the table. Maisie Fellowes and Carolina Jones stood watching proceedings with dispassionate interest, eating bananas.

Arabella Simpkin, holding her small brother Fred by the hand, accosted William indignantly.

"An' 'oo's supposed to be doin' what?" she demanded. "Not much goin' on that I can see. Sort of 'oop-la stall that William Brown *would* 'ave. All 'oops an' nothing' to 'oop."

Suddenly and for the first time William realized that no prizes were displayed on the round wooden table. He made his way to the hedge and poked his head through a convenient hole.

"Archie," he hissed, "where's the prizes?"

Archie turned a startled, bran-bespattered face in his direction.

"Aren't they there?" he said.

"No."

"They're in a brown suitcase," said Archie.

"Where?" said William.

Archie pulled out a small boy who had dived head first into the bran tub and set him on his feet before he answered.

"Oh, somewhere about," he snapped. "Use your eyes. Where's Jameson, anyway?"

But he did not wait for an answer. He had collapsed under the weight of a little girl who had jumped on to his back as he stooped to scrape up bran from the ground.

William returned to his hoop-la stall. The crowd of patrons was thicker. The angry murmurs were louder.

"Stand back there," said William in loud authoritative tones. "One at a time!'

Carolina Jones threw a banana skin at him. It caught him neatly in the right eye.

"Crumbs, where *are* the things?" said Henry impatiently. "We can't go on like this."

"In a brown suitcase," said William, dodging nimbly to avoid another banana skin.

"But where is it?" said Henry.

"He didn't say," said William. "Have a look round. Use your eyes."

Henry, Douglas and Ginger set out in search of the brown suitcase, and William turned his attention again to the patrons. But they had tired of waiting for the hoop-la stall to open and were straggling off to the Aunt Sally, the Hidden Treasure, the swings and roundabout and the Lucky Spin, leaving the hoop-la stall deserted. William collected the rings from the grass and set them in neat piles.

Suddenly Henry appeared, carrying a brown suitcase.

"Found it almost at once," he said proudly. "It was just by the hedge."

"Good!" said William.

They opened the suitcase and set out the contents—

electric razor, nail-brush, shoehorn, toothbrush, soap,
clothes-brush, hair-brush and comb, tooth-paste, talcum powder, bedroom slippers, pyjamas and dressing-
gown—ranging them at intervals over the surface of the
table. William inspected them, trying to quench a faint
spark of doubt at his heart.

"They make a jolly good show," he said.

"Funny shapes to get the rings round, some of 'em,"
said Henry.

"They have to be," said William. "It wouldn't be
any fun without it. It's called the luck of the game."

The patrons were returning. Carolina Jones had
caught sight of the display from her swing and the
news had quickly spread. They stood looking at the
prizes in silence. Even Arabella was impressed despite
herself.

"Lumme!" she said "'E ain't 'arf got some stuff,
'as 'e!"

Henry marshalled them behind the rope barrier.
William dealt out the rings at seven for sixpence.

"Stand back there!" he called. "One at a time!"

The rings hurtled wildly through the air. One hit
Henry on the nose, another perched halo-fashion on
William's head. But some found their targets. Arabella's young brother Fred, aiming at William, secured
the electric razor. Maisie Fellowes won the tooth-paste,
Carolina Jones the talcum powder, Frankie Parsons the
shoehorn, Bobby Dexter the clothes-brush. Two rings,
aimed simultaneously by the Thompson twins, came to
rest on the pyjamas. Victor Jameson's joined it.
Victor secured the jacket and the Thompson twins
started a tug of war, each holding a leg of the trousers
and pulling with all their might. The material gave way

with a dull rending sound. Jimmy Barton's ring had come to rest on the dressing-gown. He seized it with delight, put it on and marched round the stall, its skirts trailing behind him, shouting exultantly.

And then Sir Julius Egerton appeared.

His face was white with anger, his lips set, his brow overcast. Wordlessly he seized the suitcase and began to fling into it such articles as still remained on the stall. Then he looked around. Maisie Fellowes sat on the grass, squeezing the tube of tooth-paste and eating it with every appearance of enjoyment. Carolina Jones sat next her, scattering the talcum powder over a dandelion plant and observing the result with close attention.

Frankie Parsons sat on the edge of the herbaceous border digging holes in the earth with the silver shoe-horn. Fred sat next him pushing the electric razor through the soil and making train noises. Bobby Dexter was brushing the pebbles in the path into a little heap with the silver-backed hair-brush.

Sir Julius directed a glance of fury at the company, snatched the dressing-gown from Jimmy Barton and turned his attention to the Thompson twins. The legs of the pyjama suit were now attached to each other only by a couple of threads and, seeing this, Sir Julius uttered a fresh snarl of rage and aimed a blow at Launcelot that sent Geraint flying. It was at this point that William, who until now had been paralysed by surprise, found his voice.

"Here!" he said indignantly. "Stop pinchin' our hoop-la prizes."

Sir Julius turned to him and spoke through clenched teeth.

"Are *you* reponsible for this outrage?" he said.

"It's my stall," said William," an'—an' you've pinched my hoop-la prizes an'——"

"Hoop-la prizes!" exploded Sir Julius. Emotion choked him so that he had difficulty in proceeding. "Hoop-la prizes! Are you aware, you young ruffian, that I called here to open this fête at great personal inconvenience on my way to an important political meeting, that I put down my suitcase for a moment in order to be unimpeded during my speech and that when I came to retrieve it, I found this outrage perpetrated." He dived under the table, dragged out two small boys who were belabouring each other with the bedroom slippers and hurled the various articles at random into the case. "I have a train to catch in quarter of an hour's time and my taxi is at the gate. Otherwise I would sift the matter to its core and see justice done on those responsible. But be assured that I will not let the matter rest here. He slammed the lid of the case and ran home the catch. "Your parents shall hear from me immediately on my return."

They stood watching the thin tense figure, still quivering with fury, make its way to the gate and fling itself into a taxi.

"Gosh!" said William.

Then the patrons set on him.

"I *won* it, William Brown, an' you let him take it off me. You're a *thief*."

"You're a *crook*. Give me my money back, William Brown."

"Takin' the poor kid's train off 'im. I wonder you 'ad the 'eart to do it, William Brown. You wait till I've told 'is mum."

"It was a mistake," said William desperately. "I'll go'n' find out. . . . You can have your money back an'—an' I'll go'n' find out."

He went to the hedge and poked his head through the hole again.

"Archie . . ."

Archie turned his face, more heavily encrusted with bran than ever, in William's direction.

"What do you want?" he snapped. He was feeling irritable and depressed. He hadn't seen Ethel all afternoon and the bran tub was proving too much for him.

"We can't find the hoop-la prizes. Where are they?"

"I *told* you. In a brown suitcase."

"Well, it was the wrong one," said William.

"I don't know what you're talking about. Where's Jameson, anyway? Go *away*. Can't you see I'm busy?"

Slowly, reluctantly, William returned to his hoop-la stall. Then his spirits lightened.

Ginger was approaching the stall.

He carried a brown suitcase.

The patrons crowded eagerly round and he began to unpack the case. He took out several glove puppets, bunches of ribbons, half a dozen imitation eggs, a pack of playing cards, a large particoloured handkerchief, a toy mouse, a small box painted half blue, half red, and other miscellaneous objects.

"This looks more like it," said William, again trying to quench a small spark of doubt at his heart. "It's a *smashin'* hoop-la stall now."

Lady Forrester drifted by with Angelique. She was large and loosely built, with untidy white hair and a

kindly expression. Lady Forrester was bored. She had
performed the opening ceremony, but she had to stay to
judge the Children's Fancy Dress Competition and
present the prize for the Vegetable Competition. (The
prize for the Vegetable Competition was a silver cup
donated by Lieutenant-Colonel Pomeroy with the sole
object of winning it himself.) And Lady Forrester
wanted to go home. Lady Forrester was a Wild West
fan and wanted to get home in time for Ricky the
Reckless on television.

Angelique was bored, too. She had expected something exciting and out-of-the-ordinary and all she had
found so far was stalls of frilly aprons and home-made
cakes and tins of household polish. But something of
her lethargy dropped from her as she approached
William's stall. The prizes looked odd. The children
looked odd. The whole thing lacked the suggestion of
cut-and-dried correctness that hung over the rest of the
fête. She stood in the background watching. Trade was
brisk. Carolina Jones won the Punch puppet, the
Thompson twins won the Policeman and Toby. Jimmy
Barton won the playing cards. Arabella Simpkin won
the coloured box. Fred appropriated the Judy puppet
and nursed it with an air of maternal tenderness.

"Well, it's goin' all right *now*," said William with a
sigh of relief.

And then suddenly the man appeared.

He wore a clown's outfit, his face was chalked, his
mouth reddened to an all-embracing smile. But the
smile could not hide the look of fury that seemed to
draw his features together in a tight little bunch.

"How *dare* you?" he said in a high-pitched, squeaky
voice. "Kindly return my property to me at *once*."

"They're hoop-la prizes," said William indignantly. "I'm jus' about sick of people pinchin' my hoop-la prizes. You jus' leave 'em alone."

The man glared round the stall.

"Where's my Punch and Judy? Where's my Dick Whittington? Where's my Sooty, my Dick Turpin, my Tommy Tucker . . . my conjuring properties?"

"I keep *tellin'* you," said William. "People 've

"I'M JUS' ABOUT SICK OF PEOPLE PINCHIN' MY HOOP-LA PRIZES,"
SAID WILLIAM INDIGNANTLY. "YOU JUS' LEAVE 'EM ALONE."

won 'em. They're hoop-la prizes. Out of a brown suit-case."

"Brown suitcase!" said the man, his indignation rising. "*My* brown suitcase, I'd have you know. *My* brown suitcase that contained all the equipment for my puppet and conjuring show that's due to open in ten minutes' time. I just put it down—for a second or two as I intended—while I went to the assistance of the parcels tent that was in danger of collapsing. When I returned my case was gone. Someone told me it had been taken

here and, though I could hardly believe it, I came to see
for myself. My assistant is following me and——"

His assistant suddenly appeared. He was a hearty,
beefy young man who dealt with the situation in swift
efficient fashion. He cuffed the hoop-la patrons and
banged their heads together, abstracting their plunder
from them with a friendly grin on his large blunt-
featured face.

"I think I've got 'em all, boss," he said easily.
"Come on."

He rammed the things into the case and followed the
still furious little clown through the crowd.

William gazed helplessly at the empty hoop-la table.

Once more angry murmurs were arising.

"They've taken my Sooty . . . You're a *swiz*, William
Brown, that's what you are!"

"I want my dolly back!" wailed Fred.

"Lettin' 'em take 'is dolly off 'im, pore kid!" said
Arabella indignantly. "Inyuman, that's what you are,
William Brown."

"An' you can jolly well give us our money back so's
we can go somewhere else."

"All right, *take* it!" said William, emptying his
pockets on to the stall, "Take all of it, an' *go* somewhere else an' good riddance!"

But his patrons seemed loath to leave him. They
hung about the stall in a spirit of morbid curiosity,
awaiting further developments.

Again William made his way to the gap in the hedge.

"Archie!" he said. "We can't find 'em."

"Go away!" said Archie. "I've *told* you. A brown
suitcase. Isn't Jameson there, anyway? And go
away!"

William poked his head further through the hole.

"I say, Archie, what's in that basket? I bet *they're* the things for the hoop-la stall."

"Well, they're not," snapped Archie. "They're the reserve bran tub things. We've nearly finished the things we started with ... Go away and find the hoop-la things. They're in a brown suitcase. Haven't you any sense at all? Go *away!*"

"But listen, Archie——"

Desperately Archie put an outstretched palm through the hole and pushed William's face back. William overbalanced and rolled on to the grass. He sat up and remained seated for a moment or two trying—unsuccessfully—to rally his forces and form some master plan. Then he rose to his feet, to find Angelique standing a few yards away watching him. She was a thin little girl, with blue eyes, a pale freckled face and tawny curls.

"I think this fête is jolly dull," she said, "except your part."

"My part?" said William.

"Yes." She pointed to the hoop-la stall. "I've been watching your stall. It's fun."

The patrons surrounded it in a scuffling crowd. They were pummelling each other, chasing each other, jumping on to the stall and off it. Arabella raised her voice at intervals in shrill protest. Fred sat on the edge of the herbaceous border eating geraniums. It happened that a wave of summer flu had laid low a large proportion of the stall-holders and Authority was so busy filling the places of the absentees that it had not as yet had time to go its rounds and discover the highly irregular conduct of the hoop-la stall, which was screened from

D

the rest of the Vicarage garden by the tall herbaceous border.

"There ought to be things on the stall for them to throw the rings on to," explained William.

"Well, why aren't there?" asked Angelique.

"'Cause I can't find 'em," said William. "He keeps sayin' brown suitcases an' we keep findin' brown suitcases an' people keep pinchin' them off me."

"Well, try some other way," said Angelique.

"Y—yes," said William. Suddenly a light seemed to break through his sombre countenance. "*Tell* you what! He's no right to have a second helping of bran tub things before we've had a first helping of hoop-la things. We'll *get* 'em. We'll get that basket of things that he's got over there. We'll give ole Archie one in the eye."

Angelique nodded agreement. She didn't know what it was all about, but she was a child of adventurous and enterprising disposition and she liked the idea of giving ole Archie (whoever he was) one in the eye. It would be a welcome change from guessing the weight of a cake, buying raffle tickets for tea-cosies and gazing at tins of household requisites.

"All right," she said. "How do we start?"

"Well, it's no good me goin' to that hole in the hedge again. He'll be on the look-out for me an' push me back same as he did before. You'd better do it."

"Do what?" said Angelique.

"Get that basket of things for our prizes. He'll be on the look-out for me an' he won't be for you."

Angelique peered through the hedge.

"It's a big basket," she said.

"Yes," agreed William. "I bet you couldn't pull it

through the hole without spilling everything . . . *Tell* you what! I'll climb up that tree. The branch goes right over the hedge an' over the bran tub. I've got some string." He brought from his pocket a handful of assorted objects, including a length of string, then carefully detached the string from a blob of Plasticine, a liquorice bootlace, a piece of sticky paper, a crumbling dog biscuit, a couple of corks, the top off a milk bottle and the wishbone of a chicken.

"It's good string," he went on, looking at it regretfully. "I'd meant to use it for my fishin' line . . . Never mind. Now I'll climb the tree an' you crawl through the hole in the hedge to the basket without lettin' Archie see you, an' I'll lower the end of the string an' you fasten it to the handle of the basket then I'll pull it up an' bring it along the tree an' down to the hoop-la stall . . . Come on!"

He swung himself up to the lowest branch of the tree, made his way to the end of it and looked down. Angelique had scraped through the hole in the hedge and crawled to the basket of bran tub prizes. It was plain that Archie had not yet noticed her. She was holding the handles of the basket and looking up into the tree expectantly. William lowered his length of string; Angelique seized the dangling end and fastened it to the basket. William pulled.

The end of the branch was thin. It swung and swayed; it gave out a curious creaking sound. William had taken both hands from the branch in order to hoist up the basket. He wobbled wildly for a few moments, then—clawing the air and uttering a hoarse shout—he fell from the branch on to the bran tub. The bran tub seemed to turn upside down on top of him and he crawled out from under it, threw a horrified glance around, and took to his heels so swiftly that, when the bystanders recovered from their surprise, he was no-where to be seen.

He dodged round the meadow, into the Vicarage garden, back into the meadow, back into the Vicarage garden, and suddenly found himself forming part of a procession of Bo-Peeps, Little Lord Fauntleroys, Dutch boys, Dutch girls, cowboys, Indians and squaws. They were walking round in a circle. No one seemed to have noticed him, so he joined the procession as the best means of remaining unnoticed.

In the middle of the circle, at a small table, sat Lady Forrester and Mrs. Monks. Lady Forrester surveyed the circle with an air of boredom. Mrs. Monks gave each figure a piercing scrutiny and made notes in a little notebook.

"Dutch girl," said Mrs. Monks. "Correct, of course, but ordinary. Little Bo-Peep picturesque, of course, but not original. Perhaps it was a mistake to offer a prize for originality. Oliver Cromwell—shoes wrong. Night— good stars and a pretty moon, but—no, there's nothing original about Night . . ."

Suddenly Lady Forrester's air of boredom left her.

"Oh, but *look*! . . . That boy there. He's come as a bran tub. Bran all over him and little parcels stuck in his hair. *Most* original! He must have the prize for originality. What's your name, boy?"

But William had faded into the background and was making his way—dodging round stalls and stall-holders, taking short cuts or long detours as necessary—back to his hoop-la stall.

The patrons had temporarily deserted it. Only

Angelique was there, standing on guard over the bare stall and little piles of rings.

"Well, you made a nice mess of *that*!" she said severely.

"Gosh, it was the *tree*," said William. "It mus' have had some disease. Trees *do* have diseases. They look all right an' then they fall down sudden with some disease. Anyway I got a fancy dress prize."

"Where is it?" said Angelique.

"I dunno. I thought I'd better get away quick, 'case Archie was comin' after me". He crept to the hole in the hedge and reconnoitred warily. "No, it's all right. He's still pickin' up the things an' puttin' them back in the bran. There's not much bran left . . . He's scrapin' it off the earth. He's puttin' more earth than bran in the tub, but he's managin' all right."

"Yes, *he's* managing all right," said Angelique," but what about you?"

"Well, there's no one here. They've all gone."

"They'll come back," said Angelique darkly.

She was right. The patrons had scattered to the ice-cream stall, the Aunt Sally, the Hidden Treasure, the swings, roundabout and Lucky Spin, but always some irresistible attraction drew them back to the hoop-la stall.

They were bearing down on it like so many avenging furies. William looked round desperately for escape . . . and then, to his relief, saw Douglas.

Douglas was approaching from the direction of the road. He carried a brown suitcase.

"I've *got* it," he called. "It was at the bottom of the dry ditch just outside the gate, pushed into that little tunnel that goes under the gateway. No wonder it took a long time to find it! Archie should've told us where he'd put it."

"Oh well, I 'spect he put it there an' forgot where he'd put it," said William. "Archie's like that. He puts things in safe places an' then forgets where he's put them. It was a jolly good safe place, but he forgot where it was."

He opened the case. The patrons crowded round as he took out a number of small, round, brightly coloured objects made of glass.

"They're paper-weights," said Henry. "My uncle's got some."

"Well, they're jolly good things for a hoop-la stall," said William. "They're jus' about the right size for the hoops. I knew we'd find the right stuff somewhere." He threw a stern glance of disapproval at the patrons. "Some people jus' haven't any patience."

The patrons growled but were obviously impressed.

William set out the paper-weights and distributed the wooden rings.

"Stand back there!" he called imperiously. "One at a time!"

Custom was brisk. The little round paper-weights were easy targets. Then, when the game was at its height, Police-Constable Higgs wandered up to the stall. P.C. Higgs was not on duty. He wore a sports jacket, grey flannel trousers and an air of relaxation. Outside his official capacity P.C. Higgs was a simple friendly soul who liked to be on good terms with his fellow creatures. In his official capacity he had carried on an intermittent feud with the Outlaws over the years, but he still had a weak spot for them at the bottom of his heart.

"Hello, hello, hello!" he said. "What's all this?"

"It's a hoop-la stall," said William importantly. "You pay sixpence for seven hoops an' you try to get 'em over the prizes."

"And you're in charge?" said P.C. Higgs.

"Well, yes," said William, adding hastily, "jus' at present I am."

There was something convincing in William's set, earnest expression. Might as well give the little beggar the benefit of the doubt, thought P.C. Higgs. Nothing like a taste of responsibility for sobering down these young hooligans.

"They're jolly good prizes," said William.

P.C. Higgs looked at the small glass objects.

"What are they?" he said.

"They're—well, they're jus' prizes," said William vaguely. "Jus' things you win if you get a hoop round 'em."

"All right," said P.C. Higgs. "Give us a hoop and I'll have a shot."

Two of his hoops went astray, the third settled neatly down on a paper-weight.

"That's your prize," said William.

P.C. Higgs took up the trophy and inspected it dubiously.

"What do I do with it?" he said.

"You jus'—well, you jus' put it somewhere. Same as an ornament."

"I see," said P.C. Higgs, slipping it into his pocket.

"Have another try," said William.

P.C. Higgs had another try and won another paper-weight. He slipped it into his pocket with the first.

"Have another," said William.

"No, thanks," said P.C. Higgs. "Two of 'em's enough . . . Well, so long."

He stopped to light his pipe, then strolled away among the crowd, pausing to smile indulgently at each side show as he passed it. He was surprised to see Inspector Durrant of Hadley Police Force coming towards him. Inspector Durrant was obviously on duty. He wore his uniform and walked with a brisk official step.

"I thought I might run into you here, Higgs," he said. "Things are moving at Hadley."

"No!" said P.C. Higgs.

He spoke incredulously. In his experience nothing ever moved at Hadley.

"I think we're on the track of that stuff that was stolen from Sir Julius Egerton last night. That collection of paper-weights, you remember."

"Yes, I remember," said P.C. Higgs.

He still spoke without interest. His mental picture of a paper-weight was the machine in the Post Office on which parcels and packets are weighed. He could not understand why anyone should want either to collect or steal them.

"The poor chap was in an awful state about it but he had to go off as usual, opening things and making speeches—he couldn't stop even if he tried, you know—so he left us to deal with it."

"And you've dealt with it?" said P.C. Higgs.

"Well, we'd got an idea that it was that Nobby and Robinson couple and, anyway, Nobby squealed. You see, Robinson actually took the stuff and he was to have dumped Nobby's share in a hiding place they'd often used before. Bottom of the dry ditch near the Vicarage

gate under all that rough grass and stuff just where it
goes under the gateway. Rum sort of hiding place, but
they've somehow got used to it. Anyway, Nobby went
to collect his share of the swag and it wasn't there.
So he came and told us the whole yarn. Evidently it's
not the first time that Robinson has double-crossed
him. We've got Robinson and he swears that he put the
stuff there and that it was there less than an hour ago
but there's no trace of it. So keep your eyes skinned,
won't you?"

"Yes," said P.C. Higgs. "I'd better take down some
details, hadn't I? I've got my notebook somewhere."
He put his hand into his pocket and pulled out a paper-
weight. He smiled at it indulgently. "A hoop-la prize,"
he explained.

Inspector Durrant was staring at it with bulging eyes.
His usually ruddy cheeks had paled. His lips moved
silently for a few moments, then words came.

"That's one of 'em," he said. "It's the one with the
turquoise overlay. It's worth five hundred pounds."

P.C. Higgs plunged his hand into his pocket and
brought out the other. Inspector Durrant's eyes bulged
yet further, his jaw dropped, the greyish tinge of his
cheeks deepened almost to yellow.

"That's the baccarat red double overlay," he said.
"It's worth three-fifty."

"Blimey!" said P.C. Higgs faintly, 'an' I got 'em off a
hoop-la stall."

"Where?" snapped Inspector Durrant.

"Over there."

"Come on! Quick! We must get 'em back."

They got them back. There were still several of them
on the hoop-la table. The patrons who had won the

others stood round inspecting them suspiciously. Some were already demanding their money back.

"A mingy bit of coloured glass," Arabella Simpkin was saying. "Another of your swindles, that's what it is, William Brown."

"It's a *nornament*," persisted William hoarsely.

"Funniest ornament *I've* ever seen. You can gimme back my money or I'll go 'n' fetch the police." She turned sharply to find Inspector Durrant at her elbow. But it took more than that to disconcert Arabella. "I want me money back off that boy," she said, pointing to William. "'E's took sixpence off me fer a bit of rubbish not worth a ha'penny. False pretences, that's what it is. Daylight robbery as well."

"You shall have your money back and double, Miss," said Inspector Durrant.

INSPECTOR DURRANT WAS STARING WITH BULGING EYES. "THAT'S ONE OF 'EM," HE SAID. "IT'S WORTH FIVE HUNDRED POUNDS."

Gently he took the St. Louis paper-weight with green carpet ground (value £195) from her hand and put a shilling into it.

"Crikey!" said Arabella, hastily pocketing the coin. Then, afraid that her tone had betrayed her pleasure, added, "About time I got me rights, too!"

The other patrons crowded round, handing in their paper-weights, demanding their shillings in return, then scampering off to the roundabout, the swings, the Hidden Treasure, the Lucky Spin, the Aunt Sally. . . .

William had till now watched proceedings in silent amazement, but gradually amazement was giving way to resentment.

"Here! what about *me*?" he burst out indignantly. "What about my hoop-la prizes? Every single time I put 'em out someone comes an' pinches them. That ole Sir Julius sayin' it was *his* stuff an' I bet it wasn't. An' he's goin' to see our fathers about it an' I bet they'll believe him an' not us."

"I think you need have no apprehensions on that score," said Inspector Durrant when he had heard William's story. "I think you'll find that Sir Julius will be only too willing to overlook any slight inconvenience you may have caused him."

"Yes, but——" began William, then stopped.

Inspector Durrant and P.C. Higgs were already on their way to the police station.

But someone else was coming through the crowd.

It was Jameson Jameson.

He carried a brown suitcase.

Throwing a frowning glance at the empty hoop-la stall, he passed on to the hedge, addressing Archie over the top of it.

"I've come," he said.

Archie raised a weary, bran-disfigured face and gave a start of surprise.

"I thought you were there all the time," he said.

"Of course I wasn't," said Jameson curtly. "Surely you got my message. Why on earth didn't you bring the prizes with you?"

"Didn't I?" said Archie vaguely.

"No. I called at your cottage to see if there was any message and I found the case of prizes on your kitchen table."

"Oh," said Archie. He gave the subject a moment's thought and added, "I suppose I must have left it there."

"I see no other explanation," said Jameson. "Well, I'll get going."

He returned to the hoop-la stall. It was empty and unattended. After one glance at Jameson's stern resolute face, the Outlaws had decided to make their way as quickly as possible to the woods for the long postponed game of Cowboys and Indians.

The fête was over. The peace of evening had descended on the scene, showing the trampled grass and litter—ice-cream cartons, paper wrappings, banana skins and orange peel. Stall-holders were packing up the left-overs from their stalls. Workmen were dismantling roundabouts and swings.

Lady Forrester had managed to reach home in time for Ricky the Reckless. She had been persuaded with difficulty to stay to present the Vegetable Cup and even then her thoughts were so firmly fixed on Ricky that in place of the silver cup she had absently presented

Lieutenant-Colonel Pomeroy with the half-eaten ice-cream cornet that Angelique had carelessly laid on the table in front of her. The mistake had been quickly rectified and now she was comfortably ensconced in an arm-chair in front of the television set, her gaze fixed eagerly on Ricky as he galloped to the rescue of a ravishing blonde, kidnapped and held in a gloomy underground cave.

Angelique was upstairs in her bedroom writing to her mother.

"I've been to a fate. It wasn't like you said. I put the hoop-la prizes into a basket but the boy fell into the bran tub and policemen came and pinched the prizes and the boy was mad. It wasn't a bit like the ones you used to go to, but it was fun."

Archie sat with Ethel among the débris of the tea tent, drinking lemonade through a straw. Bran still adorned his hair and beard and, to a certain extent, obscured his vision, but Ethel was smiling at him kindly and for Archie, at any rate, the world was bathed in rose colour.

"It was sweet of you to take on the bran tub," Ethel was saying. "I'm sorry I hadn't time to come round and see you, but I suppose everything went all right."

"Yes, m-m-m-marvellously," beamed Archie.

Mrs. Brown was unpacking her purchases at the kitchen table when William reached home.

"Oh, there you are, dear!" said Mrs. Brown. "What have you been doing?"

"Playing Cowboys an' Indians," panted William, inspecting her purchases with interest.

"I thought you were going to the fête."

"Yes, I did," said William casting his mind back with some difficulty to the earlier events of the afternoon.

"I hope you didn't get into any mischief," said Mrs. Brown.

"Of course not," said William. "I helped at the hoop-la stall."

"That was kind of you, dear," said Mrs. Brown.

"An' I won a fancy-dress prize."

"Oh, William!" said Mrs. Brown, touched by this unexpectedly blameless record. "I didn't know you were going in for it. What did you go as?"

"A bran tub," said William.

"Oh . . ." said Mrs. Brown. "What was the prize?"

"I dunno," said William. "I forget to fetch it." He opened a paper bag that Mrs. Brown had laid on the table. "Gosh! What a lot of sausage rolls!"

"Yes, I don't know why I bought so many. They were selling them off."

"I'll eat them for you if you like," said William.

"All right, dear. They'll do for your supper. I'll go and take my things off."

When she came back William was kneeling on a chair at the kitchen table, eating sausage rolls and reading the evening paper. Most of the newsprint was obscured by crumbs, but he cleared them away as he read.

"Gosh!" he said indistinctly. "Nearly a whole page about teachers strikin'."

"It's very sad, dear," said Mrs. Brown. "I hope yours won't."

"I hope they will," said William.

"Now do go to bed, dear."

William went slowly upstairs. A little shower of bran

fell from him as he pulled off his jumper. He looked down at it in a slightly puzzled fashion. A bran tub . . . a hoop-la stall . . . He thrust his hand into his trouser pocket; his mother had given him half a crown to spend at the fête. He hadn't spent it and he hadn't got it. He'd given it away to the patrons when he returned their money.

He stood for a moment lost in thought, then his face beamed with the light of a sudden idea. He slid neatly down the balusters.

"Mother . . ."

"Oh, William!" groaned Mrs. Brown. "I thought you'd gone to bed."

"I have," said William. "I mean, I am going. But I've got a smashing idea, Mother. Listen! If they do go on strike an' we can't go to school, we ought to get unemployment pay, oughtn't we?"

"William, what nonsense!"

"Yes, but listen——" began William.

Then he looked out of the window and his mouth dropped open.

Jameson Jameson was aproaching the gate. Behind him, just turning the bend in the road, came P.C. Higgs. There was little doubt in William's mind that they were bound for the same spot. A moment's consideration told him that, with luck, the two visits would cancel each other out. But he decided to take no chances.

"Good night, Mother," he called from half-way upstairs. "I've sud'nly gone tired."

When Mrs. Brown entered his bedroom a short time later, followed by Jameson Jameson and P.C. Higgs, William was in bed and—to all appearances—fast asleep. Mrs. Brown put a finger to her lips and tiptoed silently from the room, still followed by Jameson Jameson and P.C. Higgs. Only P.C. Higgs stayed long enough to catch the eye that William opened cautiously to reconnoitre his position.

The two exchanged a solemn wink before P.C. Higgs turned to tiptoe silently down the stairs.

WILLIAM AND THE WITCH

"THERE'S goin' to be nothin' left for us to do when we grow up," said William gloomily.

"How d'you mean?" said Ginger.

"Well, they'll have *done* everythin'," said William. "They'll have climbed every mountain there is an' got on to the moon an' dug down into the middle of the earth an' come out at the other end. I bet they'll even have found the Loch Ness monster. There'll be *nothin'* left for us to do."

"There's explorin'," said Douglas after a moment's thought.

"They've explored everywhere," said William, his gloom deepening. "They've explored Egypt an' Africa an' India an' Canada. They've not even left us the North Pole or—or the Isle of Man."

"Yes," said Henry, "but those are all places that are a long way off. No one's ever thought of explorin' *near* places. I bet there's lots of *near* places that no one's explored. They jus' never think of it. They only think of places where they've got to have camps an' dogs an' sleepin' bags an' natives an' tinned milk an' things. They never think of *near* places."

The four had been driven into the old barn by a sudden shower of rain. They stood in the doorway, watching the downpour, gloomily licking the remains of ice-cream cornets.

William considered Henry's last remark in silence, then his expression lightened.

"Gosh, yes," he said, swallowing the tail end of his cornet and wiping his hands on his pullover. "Jus' think of the whole of England, the *whole* of it! Hundreds an' thousands of roads an' little lanes an' I bet no one's ever been down *all* of 'em. You don't know *what* you'd find if you started lookin' . . . It's a jolly good idea."

"What is?" said Henry.

"Startin' explorin' near places that no one's thought of explorin' before. Gosh, we might find anythin' hidin' away anywhere."

"Savages," suggested Ginger.

"Cannibals," said Douglas.

"Picts an' Scots," said Henry.

"Prehistoric monsters," said William.

"Flying saucers," said Ginger.

"We might find 'em all," said William optimistically. "Anyway, we'd better fix where we're goin' first. Let's think over all the roads round here an' see if we know where they go to."

They thought over all the roads—the roads to Hadley, to Marleigh, to Steedham, to Mellings, to Applelea . . . They were familiar roads. The Outlaws had traversed them all, times without number. They could hold no possible trace of undiscovered territory. No cannibals, savages or prehistoric animals could possibly lurk there.

"Not much good, is it?" said Henry dispiritedly.

"There might be somethin' underground," suggested Ginger. "Underground passages used by crim'nals or somethin'."

"Not very likely," said Henry.

"An' jolly dangerous," said Douglas. "I'd rather

have flyin' saucers than crim'nals any day. They stick at nothin', don't crim'nals."

There was a far-away expression on William's face.

"I'm jus' thinkin' . . ." he said slowly.

They turned to him expectantly.

"Yes?" they said.

"Well, I've jus' remembered that little lane that goes off from the Marleigh road jus' past the quarry. I've never been down it, have you?"

It turned out that the others had not been down it, either.

"I don't even know where it goes to, do you?"

It turned out that the others did not know where it went to, either.

"It hasn't got a name even."

But Henry insisted that it had got a name. It was a half-obliterated name on a ramshackle board almost hidden by the overgrown hedge, but the name was there. It was Briar Lane.

"We might start on that," said William.

"Yes, but we'd look jolly silly if we went explorin' a place that's been explored already," said Henry. "I mean, p'r'aps everyone else knows about it. P'r'aps we're the only people who've not been down it. If they all know about it we'll have to find somewhere else."

"Well, the rain's stopped," said Henry, "an' it's nearly lunch time, so I bet we all go home now."

"All right," said William, "an we'll ask our fam'lies about this Briar Lane an' we'll meet again this after-noon an' see what they've said."

It happened that, on that particular day, the whole Brown family was assembled for lunch. William made spasmodic efforts to work his way into the conversation but was firmly ejected at each attempt. Robert, who was off with the last girl-friend and not quite on with the next, sang praises of his motor-cycle, Mr. Brown recounted his morning's triumphs on the golf course, Ethel gave a slightly catty description of Dolly Clavis's new hair-do, and Mrs. Brown expressed a dark suspicion that the man who delivered the laundry had been drinking. But the steak and kidney pie was delicious, the treacle tart had the right quality of sweetness and stickiness, and it was not till William had almost finished his second helping of tart that he turned his attention to the subject of Briar Lane.

"Where does Briar Lane go to?" he said.

His voice, deep and earnest, cut through the conversation. They turned to look at him.

"What do you mean, where does Briar Lane go to?" said Mrs. Brown.

"Well, where does it go to?" said William. "It mus' go somewhere. Stands to reason. If it's a lane it mus' go *somewhere*."

"What *is* the boy talking about?" said Ethel.

Robert touched his forehead.

"Poor chap! It's not his fault."

"Don't be ridiculous," said Mrs. Brown, rising as usual to the defence of her last-born. "I know quite well what he means. Curiously enough, I've never been down Briar Lane, though it's so near. I know that it doesn't lead anywhere in particular. It just tails off into a path through the woods. I believe there's a cottage or so there, but I've never known anyone who lives there. It's not a very inviting-looking place—and knee-deep in mud in the winter."

"Come to think of it," said Mr. Brown, "I've never been down there either. Have you, Robert?"

"No, I haven't," said Robert. "I have other things to do than mooch down little mud-infested by-ways."

"I haven't been down it either," said Ethel. "There's an awful little dip at the bottom called the Hollow and then it wanders off into the wood. It's unmade-up and full of holes."

"May I go, please?" said William, swallowing the last mouthful of his treacle tart and rising hastily to his feet.

He spoke in a brisk business-like voice and had vanished from the room before anyone had time to reply.

"Well, well, well!" said Robert.

"The boy seems to have something on his mind," said Ethel.

"Can't be much," said Robert. "There wouldn't be room for much."

"Now, now, children!" said Mrs. Brown.

William had reached the old barn, where Ginger, Douglas and Henry were waiting for him.

"I asked my fam'ly an' they said they hadn't been down it," he announced breathlessly. "They said it was jus' a track leadin' into the wood."

"Mine said that, too," said Ginger.

"So did mine," said Douglas.

"So did mine," said Henry.

"Gosh!" said William. There was a note of excitement in his voice. "It *is* unexplored, then. I bet we'll go down to hist'ry explorin' it."

"We don't know *what* we're goin' to find."

"Savages," said Ginger.

"Cannibals," said Douglas.

"Picts an' Scots," said Henry.

"Flyin' saucers an' prehistoric animals," said William.

"Anyway, whatever they are, they're sure to be vi'lent so we'd better go armed."

"We'd better take provisions, too," said Henry, "'case we're cut off from civ'lisation."

"We'll get our things ready this afternoon," said William, "an' start away after tea. We'll meet in Marleigh Road at the end of the lane."

The clouds had gathered, and a lowering sky overhung the scene when the four Outlaws met at the end of Briar Lane, furnished with such arms and provisions as they had been able to assemble in the interval. William carried his air-gun, Ginger his water-pistol, Henry a complicated anti-missile device of his own invention and Douglas his bow.

"Couldn't find any arrows," he explained. "I was usin' them for masts for my boats an' they mus' have got sunk. But I bet I could push this bow over an enemy's head an' pretty near strangle him, pullin' the string tight."

"Yes, if he'd *let* you," said William. "Now, what about provisions?"

It turned out that William had brought the toast left over from breakfast and half a bottle of horseradish sauce. Henry had brought a cake that had sunk heavily in the making and that his mother wanted to get rid of. Ginger had brought a paper bag full of cold cabbage ("it'll stop us catchin' scurvy," he said), and Douglas had set out with three bananas but had absentmindedly eaten them on the way.

"Oh, well, I 'spect it'll be enough," said William. "I bet we won't have much time for eatin' food if they turn out to be savages."

"Or cannibals," said Douglas. "We'll more likely get eat'n."

"There's worse things than bein' eat'n," said William darkly. "Well, come on. I'll go first."

"No, we'll go in a row," said Henry. "If there's any danger we'll meet it together."

They stood for a moment or two, inspecting the scene before them. The lane sloped downhill, then bore sharply to the right. Tangled hedges almost met overhead. The ground was boggy and uneven.

"WELL, COME ON," SAID WILLIAM. "WE MIGHT AS WELL START OUT FOR WHATEVER IT IS."

"Well, come on," said William. "We might as well start out for whatever it is."

Keeping abreast, the four set off down the lane. William's pace quickened and Douglas's slackened as they neared the bend in the lane.

"If it's cannibals," said Douglas, "we'll jus' disappear, leavin' no trace, an' no one'll ever know what happened to us."

"Someone might find our bones," said Ginger.

"I 'spect they eat your bones," said Douglas. "I 'spect they have special teeth for eatin' bones."

"Oh, come on," said William impatiently. "Get your weapons ready."

Rounding the bend, they saw the lane dip into a hollow, where stood a tumbledown house overgrown with ivy, then dwindle to a path and disappear into the wood. They approached the house slowly and stood looking up at it. Above them the sky was almost black, and a roll of thunder sounded ominously in the distance.

As they stood there a face appeared suddenly at one of the windows. It was the face of an old woman, thin and wrinkled, with nutcracker nose and chin and straggling white hair. It seemed to vanish almost as soon as it had appeared.

"Gosh!" breathed Ginger. "A witch!"

Heavy drops of rain had begun to fall.

"Come on," said William, turning up his coat collar. "Let's get out of this."

They ran on down the lane till they reached the edge of the wood and crouched under a bush as the thunderstorm gathered force.

"I only ran away 'cause it was rainin'," said William. "I didn't run away from that ole witch."

"Anyway, it wasn't cannibals," said Douglas.

"Or savages," said Ginger.

"Or Picts an' Scots," said Henry.

"Or prehistoric monsters or flyin' saucers," said William. "It was only an' ole woman an' it couldn't be a witch 'cause there aren't any nowadays."

Another roll of thunder echoed through the wood. The rain began to fall more heavily. A flash of lightning cut across the sky. The Outlaws huddled closely together.

"I've jus' remembered somethin'," said Henry.

"What?"

"There *are* witches nowadays. A man was talkin' to my father about it las' week an' he said there *are* them. Not in big places or towns, of course, but there still are them in small remote villages, an' they carry on jus' same as they used to in the old days."

"Crumbs! She *was* one, then. I bet this is a small remote village."

"I think it's time we went home," said Douglas.

"No, we've got to find out more about this witch," said William firmly. "What 'zactly do they *do*, Henry?"

"Well, they can turn themselves into animals—cats, gen'rally—an' they can turn other people into animals. They can turn you into a cat or a mouse or a hedgehog or *anythin'* an' you can't do anythin' about it. You jus' have to *be* one. An' they can put spells on people to make everything go wrong for them. An' they can fly through the air on broomsticks an' they can send floods an' winds an' storms."

"I bet she's sendin' this one," said Ginger, turning up his coat collar to stop the rain trickling down his neck. "She was there at the window an' she mus' have seen us an' she sent this storm immediately afterwards."

"Seems like it," said William judicially. "What else do they do, Henry?"

"Lots of things," said Henry, "but I've forgotten what they are. Anyway, my father was int'rested in what that man said an' he got a book on it out of the library. It's somewhere about at home. I'll have a look at it an' see what else they do."

The rain had stopped and a few fitful gleams of sunshine escaped the heavy clouds.

"Come on," said William. "We'd better go."

"We'll have to be jolly careful passing the house," said Douglas. "S'pose she turned us into something big like elephants. We'd look jolly silly."

"Well, there's lots of int'restin' things we could do as elephants," said William.

"Oh, come *on*," said Douglas.

They approached the house slowly, turning fearful eyes on it through the dusk.

"I 'spect she's makin' herself into a cat," whispered Douglas.

They halted for a moment at the window where they had seen the old woman. The old woman was no longer there but—a black cat was sitting on the window-sill. As the Outlaws drew level with the window the cat leapt out and streaked across the path.

The four fled up the hill to the road.

"Gosh, she *had* changed herself into a cat," panted William. "She's a witch all right. That *proves* it."

"An' did you see the broomstick?" said Ginger.

Yes, even in their panic flight they had not failed to notice the besom that was propped against the wall of the house.

"Well, we've been in the jaws of death an' we're jolly lucky to have got out with our lives," said William.

"An' we won't go down there again," said Douglas. "We got mixed up with a witch once before an' it didn't do us any good."

"That was a *pretend* witch," said William, "an' this is a real one. At least, we're pretty sure she is. Anyway, we've got to find out a bit more about it. We can't jus' leave it like this."

"All right," said Henry. "I'll read this book tonight an' tell you about it tomorrow."

Dripping, muddy-footed, but filled with secret excitement, William made his way home.

"Good gracious, William!" said Mrs. Brown. "Go upstairs and wash and change at once. Need you have got into quite such a mess? Couldn't you have sheltered somewhere?"

"We did," said William portentously. "We sheltered in the jaws of death."

Mrs. Brown returned to the kitchen, shrugging helplessly, and set to work on the potatoes.

The four met together on the way to school the next morning.

"Did you read that book?" said William.

"Yes," said Henry. "It's awful, the things they do. They make wax images of people an' stick pins into them an' the people they've made wax images of an' stuck pins into pine away an' die."

"Gosh!" said William on a low note of horror. "That's the same as murder."

"Yes, but no one can *prove* it," said Henry. "They've not touched the actual *person*, you see. An' most of these witches seem quite ordin'ry people on the outside, but you always get a sort of feel of evil when you go near them."

"Seems to me they're best left alone," said Douglas.

"No, we've got to find out if she's doin' these things an'—an' stop her," said William earnestly. "We'll go there again after school an' have another look at her. 'S no good goin' armed 'cause pistols an' things aren't any use against spells. We'll go disguised so she won't know who we are." He turned to Douglas. "You needn't come if you don't want to."

"Oh, yes, I'll come," said Douglas resignedly. "If

you're all goin' to be turned into things, I don't want to be the only one left yuman."

The four assembled at the end of Briar Lane as soon as school was over. The disguises were of a modest nature, in order not to attract undue attention on the main road. William wore a moustache that he had got out of a cracker at Christmas, Ginger wore a thick woollen scarf, covering his nose and mouth, Henry a tweed fishing hat of his father's and Douglas an old nylon stocking of his mother's drawn over his face.

They stood again in a little group looking down the lane.

"My father's taken that book back to the library," said Henry," but I had another good look at it before he took it."

"Well, what do they do besides stickin' pins in images?" said William.

"If I've got to be turned into anythin'," said Douglas through his nylon stocking, "I'd rather be somethin' fierce like a lion."

"Oh, shut up," said William. "What else do they do, Henry?"

"Well, they've got things called—called familiar spirits."

"Familiar what?" said William.

"Spirits," said Henry. "They're sort of in the shapes of animals an', as far as I could make out, these witches sort of keep them as pets. I think they can set them on people an' they're invisible so people can't see 'em."

"That sounds pretty bad," said Ginger.

"'Course it is," said Henry, "an', if we don't put 'em down, they'll spread all over the country."

"We'll put 'em down all right," said William firmly, "but first we've got to find jus' what they're doin'."

"In some ways I wouldn't mind bein' a crocodile," said Douglas.

"Oh, shut *up*," said William. "Now come on. Let's go in single file an' keep near the hedge so she can't see us comin'."

"I expect she's got spies—toads an' bats an' things— keepin' a look-out all down the lane," said Ginger.

"I wouldn't like to be a bat," said Douglas. "They can't go out in the day-time."

"Sh!" said William. "I bet she can hear everything we say."

Dusk was falling and the tangled hedges seemed to shut out what light there was. A faint breeze rustled the leaves overhead and the four looked up apprehensively.

"I bet that was her goin' off on her broomstick," said William.

"It might have been a familiar spirit," said Henry.

They reached the end of the lane and stood in the shadow of the hedge. The house was in darkness.

"It *was* her," said Henry. "There's no one in the house."

"Look!" said William. "There's a light in that shed."

They turned to look at the shed that stood by the side of the house, half hidden by trees. A square of light shone through the dusk.

"That's where she is," said William, adjusting his moustache. "Come on! Let's creep along to it. Don't make a sound."

Silently, warily, they approached the shed and peered cautiously through the lighted window. Then they gave a gasp of horror. For the witch was there. She sat at a

SILENTLY, WARILY, THEY APPROACHED THE SHED AND PEERED
CAUTIOUSLY THROUGH THE LIGHTED WINDOW.

wooden table, her white wispy hair floating about her
face, her thin frame encased in a red and black overall,
hard at work. She was fashioning a human figure, her
fingers moving lightly over the pliant material, adding
a bit here, altering a bit there . . .

William had turned pale.

"Gosh!" he said. "It's got a look of my mother."

And it had . . . Though the features were indiscern-
ible, there was something vaguely suggestive of Mrs.
Brown in the set of the head and the general stance of
the figure, even in the as yet rudimentary features.

"Yes, it has a bit," agreed Henry.

William's moustache had fallen to the ground. He
stooped to pick it up, thrust it into his pocket and
pressed his face against the window in order to get a
better view. At that moment the woman looked up and
fixed piercing eyes on him.

THE WITCH SAT AT A WOODEN TABLE, HER WHITE WISPY HAIR
FLOATING ABOUT HER FACE, HARD AT WORK.

E

Without a word the Outlaws turned and fled back up the lane to the main road. There they stopped to consider the situation.

"It *was* like my mother," said William.

"There was jus' a *look* of her," admitted Ginger.

"An' she was stickin' pins into it," said William.

"We didn't actu'ly *see* her stickin' pins into it," Henry pointed out.

"No, but she was bendin' over it an' I *bet* she was stickin' pins into it," said William. His face was tensed with anxiety. "Gosh! I'd better go home an' see if my mother's all right."

"You'd better not tell her about it," said Henry. "She might go to the p'lice, same as grown-ups always want to, an' then this witch'd get mad and put some awful spell on her that we'd never be able to take off. Why, in this book I read one woman had a spell put on her that she vomited nails all over the place. Gosh! S'pose your mother started vomiting nails all over the place."

William's face took on a deeper pallor and his eyes widened in horror.

"Well, I'll go an' see how she is," he said.

"I hope you'll be in time," said Douglas, sighing heavily.

William was already running quickly down the road towards the village.

He found his mother in the kitchen unpacking the grocery order that had just arrived.

"How are you feeling, Mother?" he said anxiously.

Mrs. Brown looked at him in surprise. His solicitude was unusual and unexpected.

"Well, as a matter of fact, dear, I'm not feeling too

good," she said. "I've got a nasty cold coming on. Put the sugar in the larder, will you?"

"When did it start?" said William as he put the sugar in the larder.

"What? The cold? This evening. It came on quite suddenly as they often do," said Mrs. Brown, strangling a sneeze. "Empty this packet of tea into the caddy, dear. Of course the weather's been very treacherous."

William gave a sinister snort.

"It's not the weather that's been treacherous," he said. "Gosh! It's not the *weather*."

"Whatever do you mean, dear? Matches . . . Put them on the top shelf for me, will you? *William!* Where on earth are you off to? You've only just come in."

William's voice floated back from the garden.

"I've got to go an' see Ginger about somethin'. It's jolly important. It's a matter of life an' death."

Ginger heard the story with frowning attention.

"Yes, it's pretty serious," he agreed. "We've got to *do* somethin'! But we'd better make quite sure first."

"What d'you mean, make quite sure?" said William indignantly. "We saw her stickin' pins into it, didn't we? An' now my mother's pinin' away."

"Well, let's make *quite* sure first," said Ginger. "We didn't axshully *see* the pins an' your mother's cold may be a nat'ral one same as ordin'ry people get. I've even known the Vicar get 'em sometimes."

"Well, it isn't," said William. "That sneeze she did wasn't an ordin'ry sneeze at all. It had—it had a sort of *feel* of evil in it."

"Well, we'll go down there again after school to-morrow," said Ginger, "an' see what she's doin'."

After school the next day they walked through the

dusk to the end of Briar Lane. A mist was gathering and the dark tunnel-like lane looked less inviting than ever. Again they made their way down the lane in the shelter of the overhanging hedge.

The news of Mrs. Brown's cold had brought a chilling air of reality into the situation, though Douglas and Henry tried to take a commonsense view of things.

"We weren't *sure* it was meant to be your mother," said Henry. "An' we didn't *see* the pins."

"She might have jus' *caught* a cold," said Douglas.

"You can *catch* any sort of disease without witches."

"Oh, shut up an' come on," said William.

Again the house was in darkness. Again light streamed through the dusty window of the shed as the boys approached it slowly, cautiously, in single file. Again William's moustache fell to the ground and had to be put into his pocket. Again they peered through the window . . .

Then William gave a gasp that was almost a scream. For the figure, now glazed and coloured, that stood there on the wooden table was unmistakably the figure of Mrs. Brown. It even wore, correct to the last detail, the hat and coat that Mrs. Brown had bought in London a few weeks ago. Next to it was another figure on which the witch's fingers were busily working. It was as yet unfinished but the figure of a young girl was emerging— slender, long-legged, the head tilted slightly to one side. And—there was no doubt about it—it had a look of his sister Ethel.

Once more William pressed his face against the glass. Once more the woman looked up with a start from her work. Then she went to the door, flung it open and stood staring into the mist. The four boys crouched by the side of the shed. The woman went in and closed the door. The boys streaked up the lane to the main road, not speaking, hardly drawing breath, till they reached it.

"Gosh, she'd got my mother all right," said William.

"An' she'd nearly got Ethel," said Ginger.

"She'll be gettin' us nex' thing we know," said Douglas in a quavering voice.

"Yes, we're on the horns of a dilemma all right," said Henry.

"We're more than on the horns of it," said William solemnly. "We're in its jaws. . . . I'd better go an' see how my mother is an' if anything's happened to Ethel."

"An' you'd better be quick," said Douglas.

"I'll have to tell 'em what's happenin' now," said William. "We can't let it go on. We've got to put 'em on their guard."

"No, you can't do that," said Henry firmly. "It'd make this witch furious an' they do the awfullest things when they're furious. Why, one witch in this book sent insects all over a person's house. All *over* it. Every *inch* of it."

"I don't mind insects," said William. "I *like* 'em. But they'd drive my mother mad . . . Anyway, I'll go home now an' see how they are an' if they aren't any better we'll have to think of somethin' to do about it."

He found his mother in the sitting-room knitting a pullover for Robert. Her nose and eyes were red and she sneezed violently as he entered.

"How are you, Mother?" he said anxiously.

Again Mrs. Brown threw him a glance of surprise mingled with tenderness. She was deeply moved by his concern. After all, she thought, whatever people said of him, the boy's heart was in the right place. He might at times be rough and rude and ill-mannered, but a boy who was so concerned by a mere cold in his mother's head couldn't have much wrong with him.

"Not much better, I'm afraid, dear," she said. "It's a sort of flu, I suppose. And Ethel's caught it now. She's gone to bed. I thought it best for her to keep warm."

William sat down weakly on the nearest chair. Pallor had again invaded his ruddy countenance.

"Gosh!" he said faintly.

Mrs. Brown gave him a tremulous smile. She hadn't realised how sensitive and affectionate he was beneath his rough exterior. He was evidently deeply distressed by his sister's illness. She must try to be more patient and understanding with him.

"Don't worry, dear," she said reassuringly. "It'll just have to run its course."

"Yes, but——" began William, then stopped and hastened to the door. "I'm jus' goin' out again to see Ginger."

"Again? . . . Well, your tea's ready, so do hurry."

William went into the hall, then stood, looking down at the floor, his face stiff with horror.

"There's a spider in the hall, Mother," he called.

There was a panic in his voice. The vanguard of the insect plague. . .

"How nice, dear!" said Mrs. Brown, trying to be patient and understanding. William, she knew, was passionately interested in insects. (He had once kept an "insect collection," feeding them on bread and marmalade till only one gigantic stag beetle survived.) She

mistook the note of panic in his voice for a note of
pleasure and excitement.

William had dropped on to his knees and moved his
face close to the spider's. The spider gave him a startled
glance and scuttled away out of sight.

"Huh!" snorted William, rising to his feet. "That's
jolly suspicious, that is!"

A further search of the hall, in the course of which he
discovered only a dead fly and a comatose earwig, con-
vinced him that the plague of insects had not yet
arrived in full force. He set out for Ginger's house.
Ginger and Douglas were waiting at the gate.

"Has anythin' happened?" said Ginger.

William nodded.

"Yes," he said. "Ethel's pinin' away now. It *mus'*
have been a figure of Ethel she was makin' an' she mus'
have been stickin' pins into it. An' those insects are
startin'. There was a spider in the hall."

They considered the situation in silence for a few
moments.

"Well, anyway, she's not vomitin' nails," said Douglas at last.

"No, but she might start any minute," said William.

"An' it may've been jus' an ordin'ry spider," said
Ginger.

"It was *not* an ordin'ry spider," said William with
spirit. "It had a look on its face I've never seen on a
spider's face before. A sort of *guilty* look. It acted in a
guilty way, too."

At this point Henry arrived. He looked worried and
anxious.

"I went home to get my magnifying glass," he said.
"I thought it might be useful, pickin' up clues, an' a

friend of my mother's was there an' she was sayin' that she'd seen an ole woman standin' an' lookin' over the hedge of your garden, William. She was sort of hidin' an' peepin' over the hedge an' tryin' to see into the rooms of your house. An' she described what this ole woman looked like an' it *was* the witch, so we've *got* to do somethin' about it now."

"Gosh, yes!" agreed the others.

"We'll go there again tomorrow," said William, "an' if she's still at it we'll have to do somethin' *desp'rate*."

Next evening they met, as dusk fell, at the end of Briar Lane. They had by this time abandoned their "disguises". William's moustache had lost whatever adhesive properties it had once possessed and had given up its unequal struggle with the force of gravity, Ginger had tired of the taste of his woolly scarf, Henry's father had indignantly retrieved his fishing hat and Douglas's stocking had broken out into "ladders" in all directions.

Slowly they crept down the lane.

"She's not there tonight," said Henry, peering into the darkness.

But as he spoke the window of the shed sprang into light. They approached it silently, then stood in the shelter of the shed, craning their heads towards the window.

The gasp they gave made the woman look up quickly. For the figures were—unmistakably—those of Mrs. Brown and Ethel. There had been no doubt about Mrs. Brown's figure the night before and now there was no doubt about Ethel's. It stood there—glazed and coloured —-with Ethel's red-gold hair, Ethel's blue eyes and the yellow jumper that Ethel had been knitting for the last

three months. The figure even wore the brooch that
Mrs. Brown had given Ethel on her last birthday. The
woman had returned to her work. She was bending over
it, adding touches here and there.

"Stop it!" shouted William frantically.

The woman got up and looked out of the window,
and again William found himself staring into her face
through a pane of dusty glass. Then she went to the
door and flung it open.

"Who are you?" she called into the darkness. "What
are you doing there?"

There was no answer. The Outlaws crouched on the
farther side of the shed, huddling together, shivering
with fright.

The woman went back into the shed. The four boys
crept from their hiding place and ran swiftly up the dark
lane to the road.

"Well, we've got to do somethin' *now*," panted
William, "an' we've got to do it quick. We've no time
to waste. She was stickin' pins into Ethel all right.
She'll be pinin' away worse than ever now."

"I'm beginnin' to get a sort of pinin' feeling myself,"
said Douglas nervously.

"Oh, shut up," said William. "We've got to break
the spell. You read the book, Henry. How do you break
the spells?"

"Well, I remember one way it said in the book," said
Henry. "Scratchin' their faces. If you scratch their
faces an' draw blood you break their power."

"She wouldn't let us get near enough to scratch her
face," said William. "She'd turn us into something before we started."

"I've got a sort of toad feelin' comin' over me

already," said Douglas unhappily. "I can see the rest of me's all right, but I can't see my face. Is my face all right?"

"No, it isn't," said Ginger," an' it never was."

"Isn't there any other way, Henry?" said William.

"You can throw her into a pond," said Henry, "an she'll sink if she's innocent an' float if she's guilty."

"Well, there's no point in that," said William, "cause we know she's guilty. An' anyway she wouldn't let us get near enough to throw her into a pond. . . . *Tell* you what we'll do! We'll go an' take those wax figures away from her. If she hasn't got 'em she can't stick pins into 'em."

"But we can't go back there, William," said Douglas on a high-pitched note of protest. "It's goin' into the jaws of death."

"Sounds a bit risky," said Henry.

"You an' Douglas needn't come if you don't want to," said William. "Me an' Ginger'll go, won't we, Ginger?"

"'Course," said Ginger.

"'Course I'll go too," said Henry.

"So'll I," said Douglas miserably.

"All right," said William, "an' we'd better do it quick. The longer we stay here the more pins she'll stick in an' the more diseases Ethel an' Mother'll get. Gosh! They've prob'ly got about every disease in the med'cine book by now. Come *on!*"

"Yes, but we can't jus' go in an' take 'em," said Henry. "She's there stickin' pins into 'em . . ."

"Y—yes," said William thoughtfully. "We've got to think out a plan. . . ." Suddenly the frown cleared from his brow. "*Tell* you what! Henry an' Douglas go round to the side of the house away from the shed an' make a noise like a—what did you say they kept for pets, Henry?"

"Familiar spirits," said Henry.

"Well, you and Douglas go round to the side of the house an' make a noise like a familiar spirit——"

"What sort of noise do they make, Henry?" asked Douglas.

"I don't know," said Henry. "The book didn't say."

"I can make a smashin' noise like cats fightin'," said Douglas.

"I 'spect that'd do," said William. "Anyway, you do that an' she'll dash off to see what's the matter an' while she's away Ginger an' me'll dash into the shed an' get the images an' then we'll all meet here."

"I bet it won't come off," said Douglas.

But—miraculously as it seemed—it did.

Henry and Douglas raised ear-splitting yells and cat-calls from beyond the house, the woman rushed from the shed to investigate the uproar, Ginger and William entered the shed, took the two figures and fled back to the end of the lane, where Henry and Douglas were waiting for them.

"We did a smashin' familiar spirit noise," panted Ginger.

"Yes, an' we *got* 'em," panted William.

He opened his jacket and brought out the two figures —unmistakable likenesses of Mrs. Brown and Ethel. Douglas shrank away from them apprehensively.

"Now we've got to think what to do with 'em," said William.

"Why not smash 'em?" said Ginger.

"No," said William. "You don't know what sort of spells you'll let loose if you smash 'em."

"Take 'em home an' hide 'em," said Henry.

"I'm not havin' them in my house," said Douglas. "They mus' be full of diseases where she stuck pins into them."

"I'll take 'em home," said William, "an—*tell* you what!—I'll hide 'em in the garage till we've thought what to do with them. They can't give anythin' a disease in the garage, 'cept the car, an' it's got everythin' wrong with it it could have, so it can't make much difference."

He replaced the figures beneath his jacket and the four made their way towards the Browns' house. It was a slow and thoughtful progress.

"Do you feel any disease comin' on, William?" said Ginger.

"N—no, I don't think so," said William doubtfully.

"I wouldn't hold them so near your tummy," said Douglas. "I had tummyache las' summer with green apples an' it was ag'ny."

William hastily moved the position of the figures.

"They're a bit near your heart now, William," said Henry. "People die if their hearts stop beatin'."

Again William hastily moved the position of the figures.

"They're on your chest now, William," Ginger warned him. "You might catch whoopin'-cough from them an' if you do you'll have to go on whoopin' till May. They do. It's one of the symptoms."

"Oh, well," said William, "I mus' have got somethin' all over me by now, so it's no good worryin'."

They had reached the Browns' house. The garage doors stood open. The garage was empty.

"Good!" said William. "Dad's not back from his

committee meetin' yet. Now let's find a good place to hide them."

They entered the garage and looked round. A wooden packing-case stood in the corner. William set the figures on the floor and drew some paper out of the packing-case.

"Yes, it's empty," he said. He took the figures and placed them in the packing-case, covering them with the paper.

"They can't do any harm to anyone there," he said, "so we'll leave 'em till we've thought what to do with 'em." He chuckled. "Jus' think of her goin' into that shed with all those pins an' findin' nothin' to stick 'em into. Gosh! She'll be mad. . . . Well, I'd better go an' see how Mother an' Ethel are."

He entered the house and emerged from it after a few minutes.

"They're cured already," he said. "Ethel's got up an' Mother says she feels all right."

"Well, I'm jus' about sick of it all," said Ginger. "Come on! Let's go campin' in the wood."

The next day was Saturday and the four met immediately after breakfast to discuss the situation.

"Let's go 'n' have a look at 'em," said Ginger. "They may've turned into somethin' else by now."

"Toads or crocodiles or somethin'," said Douglas.

They went into the garage, pulled out the packing-case and removed the paper.

The box was empty.

"Gosh! They've gone," gasped William. "I looked at 'em soon as I got up an' they were all right then. What'll we do about it?"

"GOSH! THEY'VE GONE," GASPED WILLIAM.

"If she's got 'em back she'll be jabbin' pins all over 'em," said Ginger. "You'd better go an' see what's happened to your mother an' Ethel."

William re-entered the house. His mother and Ethel were still at the breakfast table.

"How are you, Mother?" said William.

"Perfectly all right, dear," said Mrs. Brown. There was a hint of impatience in her voice. She was beginning to find William's constant inquiries about her health a little wearing, though she still tried to be patient and understanding. "I told you before breakfast that I was perfectly all right."

"Yes, but——" began William and stopped.

He had glanced out of the window and his face was stiffening in horror. The witch was walking slowly up the path. Her hair was tidier than it had been in the shed, and she wore a hat and a tweed suit instead of the red and black overall. But it was certainly the witch.

Mrs. Brown followed the direction of his eyes.

"Who on *earth* is that?" she said. She turned to Ethel. "Do you know who it is, Ethel?"

Ethel looked confused, almost embarrassed.

"It's Miss Tyrral," she said. "You see——"

She was interrupted by a prolonged pealing of the front door bell. Mrs. Brown went to answer it. The woman swept into the room and confronted Ethel.

"They've gone," she said dramatically. "They've been stolen."

William made a sound between a gasp and a grunt, but no one noticed him. He was hovering in the open doorway, prepared for instant flight, but held to the spot by curiosity and bewilderment.

"Be careful," he said. "She's a——"

"What have been stolen?" interrupted Mrs. Brown.

"The figures," said the woman.

"Look out!" said William. "She's been stickin'——"

"What figures?" said Mrs. Brown.

"She'll turn you into——" began William.

"Please explain this, somebody," said Mrs. Brown.

"Yes, I will," said Ethel. "Do sit down, Miss Tyrral. . . . You see, Mother, Miss Tyrral's taken an old house at the bottom of Briar Lane. It was odd that when William asked none of us knew anything about the place, but the very next day I met Miss Tyrral. She's an artist who models figures in clay and her work is famous." Miss Tyrral acknowledged this tribute with a graceful inclination of her head. "She had a show in London last year and got wonderful notices. But she's taken this isolated house because she wants to get away from people and devote herself entirely to her work."

"There are times when an artist craves solitude," said Miss Tyrral.

"Yes . . . anyway, you know it's Father's birthday next week and I thought it would be marvellous if I could get her to do a figure of you for me to give him as a present. Of course I didn't tell a soul because I wanted it to be a dead secret, but I gave Miss Tyrral all the snapshots I could find and she did quite a lot of snooping round on her own."

"Yes, indeed," said Miss Tyrral with a smile. "The situation appealed to me. I felt like a cloak-and-dagger conspirator skulking round your premises and spying on you through your windows."

"And then," said Ethel, "she suddenly decided that she wanted to do me, too."

"Yes," said Miss Tyrral. She turned to Mrs. Brown. "I felt your daughter's colouring to be a sort of challenge and I flattered myself that I'd not been unsuccessful. And then——" She stopped.

"Yes?" said Mrs. Brown. "What happened?"

Dimly William realised that the moment for flight had arrived but he still felt incapable of movement or action. He just gazed at the visitor in fascinated horror.

"Well"—Miss Tyrral sank her voice to a mysterious whisper—"last night a most extraordinary thing happened. I was working in my shed when I heard one of the most ghastly sounds I've ever heard. A sort of banshee wail. Blood-curdling and indescribably evil. I ran round to the place where it seemed to come from and—there was no one to be seen. But the *evil* seemed to hang about the place. I felt *shaken* somehow and went straight to bed. And this morning, when I went to the shed to continue working on the figures, I found them gone."

"But why should anyone steal them?" said Mrs. Brown.

"Why indeed?" said Miss Tyrral. "The whole thing is most mysterious." Again she sank her voice to a whisper and glanced cautiously around. "Have you—have you ever noticed anything *strange* about the place?"

"What place?"

"The Hollow. The spot where Briar Lane dips into the bottom of the valley before it joins the woods."

"Actually I've never been there. How do you mean, strange?"

"Evil," said Miss Tyrral earnestly. "I'm not superstitious, but some very curious things have happened there. I began to notice it especially after I got a book from Hadley library. The book was on witchcraft but there was a chapter on what they called earth spirits. In appearance, it seems, they are like stunted human beings and they are inexpressibly evil. And—you must believe me—one of them haunts the Hollow. I've seen its evil face pressed against the window staring into mine, and when I went out, no one was there. I've *felt* the evil hanging like a cloud over the place and last night"—she shuddered—"Oh, that banshee wail came from no human throat. And now the disappearance of those figures. . . ."

"Don't worry about that," said Mrs. Brown vaguely.

"It's *you* I'm worrying about," said Miss Tyrral. Again she sank her voice till it was almost inaudible. "Those creatures have powers of witchcraft. And once the *image* of anyone has come into their hands they can inflict disasters of every kind on the person." Again she shuddered. "If you'd seen the *face* that met mine through the window——"

William began to edge his way from the room, but it was too late. Miss Tyrral had not noticed him till this minute. Now, turning sharply and meeting his scowling gaze, she gave a cry of terror.

"It's here!" she cried. "It's in the house. It must have followed me. *Look* at it! It will infest your house now as well as mine. It——"

At this point Mr. Brown entered. He greeted the visitor, then turned to his wife.

"By the way, my dear, Miss Milton came and collected those china ornaments from the garage."

"What china ornaments?" said Mrs. Brown.

William had almost reached the front door but again

curiosity drew him back to hover uneasily on the threshold. He stood out of Miss Tyrral's line of vision. She gaped around, blinking distractedly.

"It's vanished," she said. "It was here. I saw it quite distinctly. And now it's vanished."

"I didn't leave any ornaments in any box for anyone," said Mrs. Brown.

"Didn't you? Well, she came along just as I was starting the car and said you'd promised to put out something for her Bring and Buy Sale."

"Oh, dear! I completely forgot about it," said Mrs. Brown.

"I told her you'd put the last lot of Sale of Work stuff in the box in the garage to be collected in case you were out and the old girl looked in and found these two china ornaments. and took them off."

"China ornaments. . . ?" said Mrs. Brown. "Could they possibly . . . ?"

"What were they like?" said Miss Tyrral.

"Just china ornaments. I remember that one had a hat on and one hadn't."

"Good Heavens! But how could they have got there? Ring up Miss Milton, Ethel."

Ethel rang up Miss Milton. Yes, Miss Milton had taken two figures from the Browns' garage, thinking that they had been put there for her Bring and Buy Sale. No, she couldn't describe them. She hadn't really noticed them. She had enough on her mind without noticing the details of china ornaments. They were just china ornaments. And someone had bought them almost at once. No, she didn't know who it was. The affair was supposed to be a coffee Bring and Buy Sale, but people started coming soon after nine and things had got a little out of hand. And she must run away now because Mrs. Bott had just arrived bringing a carpet-sweeper that was out of order and that she was sure no one would want to buy.

At this moment William's paralysis left him and he made a dash for the front door. But Mr. Brown's hand closed on his shoulder and drew him back into the room.

"Do you know anything about this, William?" he said.

William's explanation was lengthy and incoherent but somehow they gathered the gist of it.

Miss Tyrral's face broke into laughter.

"So it was *you* all the time, not an earth spirit."

"An' it was you, not a witch," said William half regretfully.

"But where are the figures?" said Ethel. "After all the trouble we took over them where *are* they?"

And then Miss Thompson entered. Smiling coyly she drew the two figures from her bag.

"I expect it's rather silly of me," she said with a little giggle, "but I bought these at Miss Milton's Bring and Buy Sale. I thought—I'm short-sighted and I hadn't my glasses with me—but I thought there was just a *look* of Mrs. Brown and Ethel about them and I thought it might amuse you, so I brought them along as a little present." She peered shortsightedly at the figures. "There *is* a faint look of them, isn't there, or am I mistaken?"

"You are not mistaken," said Mr. Brown.

"There is more than a faint look, I hope," said Miss Tyrral dryly.

"Thank you so much," said Mrs. Brown. "It's sweet of you."

Miss Thompson departed, chirruping happily to herself, and the Browns and Miss Tyrral were left alone. Miss Tyrral was gazing intently at William.

"Do you know," she said, "I'd like to model you. I've never modelled a boy before. I'd like to model you just as you are—dirty, tousled, unkempt . . ."

"He looks quite nice in his new suit," said Mrs. Brown a little coldly.

Mr. Brown chuckled.

"I was wondering what punishment to give you for your outrageous behaviour, William, but Fate has provided the answer. You shall be modelled."

William sat perched on a stool in Miss Tyrral's studio. Miss Tyrral stood at the table modelling with frowning concentration.

"I wish you'd keep still, boy," she said. "You're never still for a second."

"Well, I've got to breathe," said William irritably, "an' I've got to use my muscles or I'd lose the use of 'em. People do if they don't use 'em." He thought deeply for a few moments, then continued, "It's cows you ought to be doin', not me. Cows stay still in fields for hours an' *hours* jus' lyin' there an' thinkin'. Why don't you stop doin' me an' do a cow?"

A sudden look of interest had come into Miss Tyrral's face.

"Do you know," she said, "it's just occurred to me. I've never modelled an animal. I don't know why. I'd rather like to try. But something more exciting than a cow."

"A lion," suggested William. "Or a tiger."

"Yes . . . I could study them at the Zoo, of course."

"Or in a circus," said William. "They're more excitin' in a circus."

"Yes . . . There's one on at Olympia now, I believe, isn't there?"

"Yes," said William.

"I could go to it. But one would feel a little odd going without a child. Perhaps you'd be willing to go with me?"

William stared at her open-mouthed.

"Me?" he said. "*Gosh*, yes. *Thanks*."

"Well, I needn't keep you any longer now. I think I've got everything I need."

Dazed with rapture, William staggered out into the sunshine.

Ginger was passing the end of the lane. He held a bottle of raspberry fizz to his mouth.

"Hello," he said as he lowered it. "I came along to find you. I got this at Bentley's. We'll have swallows in turns. I've had one."

He handed the bottle to William.

"Thanks," said William. He took a long deep draught and handed the bottle back to Ginger. "I'm goin' to the circus."

Ginger stared at him, the bottle held half-way to his lips.

"Who's takin' you?"

"Miss Tyrral."

"Gosh!" There was a silence, broken only by the loud gulping sound of Ginger's swallow. Then, "How did you get her to do that?"

William shrugged nonchalantly.

"I guess I put a spell on her," he said.

MRS. BOTT AND THE PORTRAIT

"WE ought to have some ancestors, Botty," said Mrs. Bott.

"We've got 'em, dear," said Mr. Bott after a moment's thought. "We must have. Come to think of it, we shouldn't be here now if we'd not."

"Yes, but I mean we ought to get their portraits painted," said Mrs. Bott.

"It's a bit late in the day for that, love," said Mr. Bott after another moment's thought.

"All the best people have 'em," said Mrs. Bott. "'Angin' round the rooms in frames. *H*angin'. In fancy dress. Suits of armour an' suchlike. Bustles an' tights an' things."

Mr. Bott looked guardedly at his wife. Her social ambitions were apt to lead her and him into strange and unforeseen situations.

"I dunno . . ." he said doubtfully. "I think it's too late once they're dead."

"I don't see why it should be," said Mrs. Bott. Opposition always had the effect of hardening her resolution. "Anyone can paint suits of armour an' tights an' bustles an' things an' put faces to 'em. You only want a painter an' there's plenty of *them* about."

"There might be some difficulty about the faces," said Mr. Bott. "I mean, a painter's got to have a face to paint a face from, if you see what I mean, an' we don't know what our ancestors' faces looked like. It's the face that'd be the difficulty."

Mrs. Bott's brow clouded over, then cleared suddenly. "*Tell* you what, Botty! They could have mine."

"Your what, love?" said Mr. Bott, mystified.

"Face," said Mrs. Bott. "They could all have my face. Well, if they're ancestors they must've looked like us, mustn't they? The women can have my face an' the men yours." She beamed at him triumphantly. "That's an idea, isn't it? We'll have our faces in suits of armour an' tights an' bustles an' things hangin' on the wall, same as they do at Marleigh Manor an' places. You can't be a real high-up, Botty, without ancestors an' what's the use of us havin' all this money if we can't be real high-ups?"

Mr. Bott sighed. He had suspected for some time that his wife was due for another outbreak of social ambition. She would jog along happily and contentedly for months and then suddenly the fit would be on her and his peace of mind would be shattered till it had passed and she had quietened down again. The last time it had been a 'write-up' in the *Hadley Times*. Now it was ancestors. He was a simple, unassuming little man and at times he almost found it in his heart to regret the flash of inspiration by which he had invented a sauce that had transformed him from a small back-street grocer to owner of the Hall with its billiard room, library, ten bedrooms, commanding prospect and extensive grounds.

"Big gold frames," said Mrs. Bott dreamily. "All

over the wall. Our faces in suits of armour an' bustles an' tights an' things." Her ambition took wilder flights. "I don't see why we shouldn't go back to the beginning, Botty, an' start as Ancient Britons. In skins."

Mr. Bott shuddered inwardly but he knew better than to oppose the suggestion. He summoned all his diplomacy to his aid.

"There's that new wallpaper," he said thoughtfully. "Pity to cover it up before anyone's hardly seen it."

The point went home. Something of Mrs. Bott's glow faded.

"Well, yes," she admitted. "Cost a pretty penny, too, didn't it? Those gold flowers in it, raised up, like. Yes, it would be a pity to 'ide it away. *H*ide."

Mr. Bott hastened to pursue his advantage.

"You know, love, I don't think I want your face *wholesale*, as it were. All over the place. In skins an' bustles an' suchlike. I feel it'd *worry* me, somehow. Now what I'd like is one nice portrait of you as you are now. That's what I'd like, love. Just one nice portrait of you as you are now. You'd make a lovely picture. I'd—well, I'd get real pleasure from it."

Mrs. Bott was touched. She smiled coyly.

"Oh, well," she said, "if you feel like that, Botty . . ."

"I do," said Mr. Bott. "Just a portrait of you as you are now. That's what I'd like, love."

"With you, Botty," said Mrs. Bott.

"No," said Mr. Bott firmly. "Not with me. I couldn't. I'm too busy. I couldn't give my mind to it. I spoilt all those snapshots you took in the summer, remember."

"Yes, you did," agreed Mrs. Bott. "You kept movin'. You'd prob'ly move when he was doin' this portrait of you an' it'd be all out of focus same as the snapshots were. But—I'd like to have you in it, Botty. I'd feel kind of lonely all by myself."

"There's Vi'let Elizabeth," said Mr. Bott.

"Yes, of course," said Mrs. Bott, pleased by the suggestion. "Me an' Vi'let Elizabeth. Mother an' child." A thoughtful look came over her face. "I hope she'll take to bein' done."

"Yes, let's hope she will," said Mr. Bott.

"If she won't, I s'pose it's off."

"I s'pose so," said Mr. Bott. "She's that obstinate."

"It's character, Botty," said Mrs. Bott reproach-fully, "not obstinacy. It's character the child's got. An' you can't force it. I went to a talk about it at the Women's Institute. A child's got to 'ave self-expression. *H*ave. If you force a child to do what it doesn't want to it gets exhibitions an' it's bad for it."

"I think you've got the wrong word, love," said Mr. Bott. "I think it's inhibitions, not exhibitions."

"Well, in or ex, she'd get 'em," said Mrs. Bott, "so it's no use tryin' to force her. We'll see 'ow she takes to it. *H*ow. An' then we've got to find a painter."

"There's Archie Mannister," said Mr. Bott. "He's local talent. It's a good thing to employ local talent when you can."

Their minds went to Archie Mannister, the unsuccess-ful artist who inhabited a tumble-down cottage at the farther end of the village.

"He's local, of course, but I dunno about talent," said Mrs. Bott. "I've never seen anythin' he's painted that looked like what it was."

"Well, he's got to learn," said Mr. Bott indulgently. "He may've improved since the las' thing you saw."

"And he may not," said Mrs. Bott. "But—Botty, I've just remembered somethin'."

"What, love?"

"I met Mrs. Lane in the Post Office the other day and she said that she's got a nephew that's an art student comin' to stay with her nex' week. He's not as local as what Archie Mannister is, of course, but he may 'ave more talent. P'r'aps we'd better wait till we see what he's like. There's no 'urry. *H*urry."

At that moment Violet Elizabeth passed the french window. She strolled in a leisurely fashion, licking an ice lolly that was sending generous drippings down the front of her frock.

"Come in, love," said Mrs. Bott, opening the glass door.

Violet Elizabeth entered, still in a leisurely fashion, still licking the ice lolly that now sent generous drippings on to the polished parquet floor. She surveyed her parents without interest.

"Would you like to have your portrait done, love?" said Mrs. Bott.

Violet Elizabeth's small red tongue performed an adroit circular lick that encompassed the entire surface of her ice lolly.

"Will you give me a nithe prethent if I do?" she said.

For all her air of angelic sweetness Violet Elizabeth was a calculating child.

"We'll see," said Mrs. Bott. "We'll see if you're a good little girl and sit still."

"I don't want to thit thtill," said Violet Elizabeth.

She gave another circular lick to the lolly and the

remaining fragment detached itself from the stick and fell on to the parquet floor.

"Pick that up," said Mr. Bott.

"I don't want to pick it up," said Violet Elizabeth. "I'll thquath it."

She ground the piece of ice into the parquet with a miniature sandal.

"Now don't give 'er exhibitions, Botty," said Mrs. Bott, seeing an expostulation quivering on her husband's tongue.

"She's givin' 'em me," said Mr. Bott.

Violet Elizabeth licked the wooden stick clean then put it among her curls behind her ear and turned her attention to the subject under discussion.

"Who'th going to paint it?" she said.

"Well, that's the question, love," said Mrs. Bott. "There's Archie Mannister and there's this nephew of Mrs. Lane's that's coming to stay with her. Seems he's an artist, too. So we've got to make up our minds between them."

Violet Elizabeth fixed limpid blue eyes on her parent. They held their usual expression of wondering innocence, but her mind was working quickly. She was not an unintelligent child and she saw the possibilities of the situation.

Those youthful desperadoes, known as the Outlaws— William, Ginger, Henry and Douglas—used Archie's cottage and garden as their playground. Archie was so vague and absent-minded that they could turn his garden into a Red Indian camp, raid his larder, use his studio as the cockpit of an aeroplane without his even realising that they were present. There were occasions when he suddenly noticed them and drove them in

exasperation from the scene, but the occasions were
few. The result was that William and his friends
cherished for Archie a deep and ardent loyalty. They
would, Violet Elizabeth knew, go to any lengths to
secure the portrait commission for Archie. And it was
the greatest desire of her heart to be accepted by the
Outlaws as their playmate, to join in their games and
accompany them on their lawless expeditions over the
countryside.

So far all her efforts had been in vain. They continued to treat her with contempt and derision, to eject
her when she tried to join them, to ignore her threats,
her tears, her blandishments. And suddenly she saw a
way of gaining her ends. The fact that Archie's rival
was a member of the Lane family added piquancy to
the situation. For Hubert Lane was William's inveter-
ate foe. She would be able to play one off against the
other to her heart's content.

"Now will you promise to be a good little girl and
have your portrait done?" coaxed Mrs. Bott. "Then
I'll give you a *lovely* present."

But Violet Elizabeth had lost interest in the present.
She was after bigger game. She maintained her air of
wondering innocence.

"I will if it'th a *nithe* painter," she stipulated. "I
couldn't thit thtill if it wathn't a nithe one."

"Well, as I said, it's either Archie Mannister or Mrs.
Lane's nephew," said Mrs. Bott. "I expect they're both
nice."

"Can I choothe?" said Violet Elizabeth. "I'll thit
thtill if I can choothe."

"Yes, love. I don't see why you shouldn't," said Mrs.
Bott.

"I won't thtit thill if I can't choothe," said Violet Elizabeth.

There was a wistful expression on the small angelic face. Mrs. Bott knew that wistful expression and the six-year-old ruthlessness and determination that lay behind it.

"Very well, love," she said.

"Can I go now?" said Violet Elizabeth. "I want to thtart choothing."

"Very well, love," said Mrs. Bott.

Drunk with the sense of power, Violet Elizabeth gambolled gleefully through the french window.

"Sweet little thing, isn't she?" said Mrs. Bott fondly.

"Sweet," said Mr. Bott.

And the situation developed exactly along the lines for which Violet Elizabeth had hoped.

Tarquin Lane turned out to be a large athletic young man with a startlingly luxuriant moustache. It sprang buoyantly from his upper lip, took a sudden downward curve, then swung upwards with an air of careless bravado. The rest of his face was in keeping with its ornament—a prominent nose, a jutting chin, bushy eyebrows and thick, well-greased hair.

Beside it, Archie's thin harassed-looking face with its sketchy, indeterminate beard was painfully insignificant. Archie felt a pang of envy whenever the moustache came within his range of vision. He had once had a shot at a moustache himself but nothing had come of it.

As soon as Tarquin joined the Lane household, Violet Elizabeth began her plan of campaign. The news soon leaked out in the neighbourhood that Mrs. Bott and Violet Elizabeth were to have their portraits painted and that the choice of artist had been left to Violet Elizabeth.

William accosted her at the gates of the Hall.

"Archie's a *jolly* good artist, Violet Elizabeth," he said. "Gosh! He's as good as any of those ancient ones that people make such a fuss about an' put in museums an' places. Gosh! If you got your portrait painted by Archie you'd be famous all over the world. People would come from—from *America* to see it. There'd be *books* written about it. He's the best artist in the whole world, only he's not had a proper chance yet. You'll be jolly sorry if you don't have him. Huh! You'll live to rue the day."

Violet Elizabeth gave him a smile of radiant sweetness.

"I'd like to come and play Red Indianth in the woodth with you, William," she said.

William swallowed his pride with an effort.

"All right," he said ungraciously. "You can come tomorrow."

The next time Violet Elizabeth emerged from the Hall gates Hubert Lane was waiting for her. Hubert was fat and smug with a large oily smile. He carried a box of chocolates.

"I thought you'd like these, Violet Elizabeth," he said, baring his teeth in the oily smile. "They're the most expensive in the shop."

Violet Elizabeth fluttered her eyelashes at him.

"Thank you, Hubert," she said. "It'th very kind of you."

"You know my cousin's come to stay with us," said Hubert.

Violet Elizabeth fluttered her eyelashes again.

"HE'S THE BEST ARTIST IN THE WHOLE WORLD," SAID WILLIAM, "ONLY HE'S NOT HAD A PROPER CHANCE YET."

"Yeth, Hubert," she said.

"Well, he's the best portrait painter in England," said Hubert. "You—you'd be *mad* not to choose him to paint your portrait, Violet Elizabeth."

"Yeth, Hubert," said Violet Elizabeth.

"He's painted the Queen and the Prime Minister and the Archbishop of Canterbury," said Hubert, throwing truth recklessly to the winds. "You're jolly lucky to get the chance of him, Violet Elizabeth."

"Yeth, Hubert," said Violet Elizabeth.

"He doesn't do just anyone, Violet Elizabeth. He's jolly partic'lar who he paints. He's been asked to paint——" He racked his brains for something suitably sensational "—*murderers* an' turned them down. He's been asked to paint *engine drivers* an' turned them down. But I think he'd paint this portrait of you if you asked him, an' you'd be jolly lucky if he did."

"Yeth, Hubert," said Violet Elizabeth. She fixed her innocent gaze on him. "Thank you for the chocolatth, Hubert. I like chocolatth, Hubert. An' I like lolly-popth and caramelth and pear dropth and thugar mithe and jelly babieth and candy floth."

Then, holding her box of chocolates under her arm, she tripped lightly on her way.

There followed for Violet Elizabeth a period of bliss that surpassed her wildest dreams. The lust for power

"HE'S PAINTED THE QUEEN AND THE PRIME MINISTER AND THE ARCHBISHOP OF CANTERBURY," SAID HUBERT.

F

that lives in every six-year-old breast found ample and almost incredible outlet. As William's squaw she bossed and bullied and nagged and tormented. There were times when the Outlaws' loyalty to Archie was strained almost to breaking point, but they held on doggedly.

"Once this ole portrait's finished," said William, "we'll never speak to her again all the rest of our lives."

"It's not started yet," Douglas reminded him.

And every day found Hubert waiting at the gates of the Hall with his offering of chocolates or caramels or lollypops or jelly babies.

Violet Elizabeth, aware that such a situation might never occur again, dragged it out to its utmost length.

"You thaid I could choothe," she said to her mother, "and I haven't chothen yet."

"Well, you'd better be quick, love," said Mrs. Bott. "We can't keep it 'angin' on for ever. Tarquin'll be goin' 'ome soon. *H*angin'. *H*ome."

"You'll have to wait till I've chothen," said Violet Elizabeth serenely.

The artists themselves were not idle. Each of them, after furtively studying their possible subject, made experimental sketches of her. Neither bore much resemblance to the original. Tarquin's had a vague look of Mrs. Gamp and Archie's a vague look of Mr. Pickwick.

Nor was Mrs. Bott idle. She paid visits to both artists and put them through their paces.

Tarquin received her in the Lanes' heavily uphol-stered sitting-room, with Hubert lurking in the back-ground, smiling his oily smile.

"Mind you, I don't know I'm goin' to have you," said Mrs. Bott. "It depends on Vi'let Elizabeth. She's choosin' on account of havin' to have this self-expression 'cause of these complexions in her subconscious, same as this woman said at the W.I. But I thought I'd like to find out 'ow you thought you'd do me—*how*—if you did do me."

Tarquin showed her his sketch of Mrs. Gamp. Her flabby little mouth tightened.

"An' 'oo's *this* meant to be, may I harsk?" she said grimly. "Not me, I 'ope. *H*ope."

"Oh, no," said Tarquin hastily. "A friend. A mere friend."

"Well, Botty says he wants a portrait of me just as I am."

"Ah, yes," said Tarquin, raising a hand to caress his moustache. "Yes, I'd like to discuss that with you if I may. I always aim at showing the *character* of my sitters. I flatter myself that I'm a good judge of character. As I look at a person their *character* seems to spring out at me, as it were. And that's what I try to get down on to canvas."

"An' what would you say was my character?" said Mrs. Bott with ingenuous interest.

Tarquin fixed his eyes on her in what he hoped was a keen and penetrating gaze.

"Charm," he said.

Mrs. Bott bridled.

"Well, maybe," she said coyly. "Botty always said it was my winning ways that made 'im take to me. An' what else d'you see?"

Tarquin looked at the podgy little form and drew a deep breath. He might as well go the whole hog while

"AN' 'OO'S *THIS* MEANT TO BE, MAY I HARSK?" SHE SAID GRIMLY.
"NOT ME, I 'OPE. *H*OPE."

he was about it. He intensified the deep and penetrating gaze.

"Intelligence of a high order," he said. "Nobility,
sensitiveness, integrity, generosity, broad-mindedness,
culture, idealism, courage, honesty, capability and—
and charm. Above all, charm."

He stopped for breath. A sound that was almost a
purr emanated from Mrs. Bott.

"You've got me a treat," she said. "I had me crystal
gazed on the pier at Brighton last summer an' she
didn't get me 'arf as well as what you've done. Could
you put all that in me portrait at one go?"

"Indeed I could," said Tarquin, adding recklessly, "and more."

"I shouldn't have thought it showed to that extent," said Mrs. Bott, stealing a complacent glance at her reflection in the looking-glass that hung on the wall. "You must 'ave the seeing eye."

"Oh, yes, I think I have," said Tarquin. He felt that his keen and penetrating gaze was acquiring a touch of ferocity and blinked several times in quick succession. "I have that sense of the psychic that is so necessary to an artist. And I'd like to hand you down to posterity just as I see you."

"Well, I never!" said Mrs. Bott, deeply impressed. Still looking at him in a fascinated manner, she rose and gathered up her belongings. "Well, I'd better be goin' now. If it depended on me I'd say, paint me right off, but I've promised to let Violet Elizabeth choose. If she dilly-dallies too long, of course, I'll 'ave to take a hand, but—well, anyway I'll let you know definite soon as she chooses."

"Thank you," said Tarquin. "I won't worry. There's a strong suggestion of a sense of justice in the lines of your lips."

"Fancy that, now!" said Mrs. Bott. "I shouldn't have thought all that could show in just a few inches of face, so to speak, but—there you are! An' it's nice to know one's out of the ordin'ry."

"You're certainly that," said Tarquin with a ring of truth in his voice.

The sense of justice so unexpectedly revealed to her urged Mrs. Bott to pay a call at Archie's cottage on her way home. Might as well give him a chance, she thought. After all, fair's fair.

She found Archie clearing up his studio in a vague ineffectual fashion and looking for a tube of gamboge yellow that he wanted for a sunset.

Chaos accumulated in Archie's studio till he lost something and then he tidied it up by the simple process of moving everything from the place where it was to a different and equally inappropriate place. He hastily cleared a chair for his visitor, removing from it a paint brush, a palette, a tube of cobalt blue, a pair of socks, a tin opener, a mug of coffee and a nail file.

Mrs. Bott sat down gingerly and fixed him with a stony stare.

"About this here portrait," she began. "I'm lettin' Vi'let Elizabeth choose but I thought I'd better find out 'ow you're thinkin' of doin' me, if you *do* do me, that is."

Archie showed her his sketch of Mr. Pickwick. Her brow darkened as she studied it.

"And 'oo's this meant to be?" she said.

"You," said Archie simply.

"Well, you can put it right out of your 'ead—*h*ead —and 'ave another think," said Mrs. Bott tartly. "If you s'pose I'm goin' to be 'anded down to prosperity— *h*anded—lookin' like an 'arf-witted monkey you're very much mistook."

"Yes, yes," said Archie, looking round in a distraught fashion. "Of course . . . I'd no idea . . . I'm terribly sorry . . . I never for a moment intended . . . I——"

Mrs. Bott interrupted him.

"Botty wants a portrait of me just as I am. You're— you're psychic, I take it? I mean, you can't be a painter without bein' psychic. Stands to reason."

"Well—er——" said the goaded Archie, "I've never

given much thought to it. I must admit that I've never actually *seen* anything. Anything that wasn't there, I mean. I——"

"Well, you can see what's *there*, I suppose," said Mrs. Bott impatiently. "Now look at my face an' tell me honest what you see."

Archie fixed his harassed gaze on the small round countenance. He was a simple earnest soul with no thought but to answer his visitor's question as truthfully as he could.

"It's fat," he said.

"Oh, yes?" said Mrs. Bott, coldly.

"It's got a double chin. Well, three, actually."

"Oh, yes?" said Mrs. Bott menacingly.

"The eyes rather small and a little pouched," said Archie, still studying the features before him, his mind occupied solely with the problem of conveying them on to canvas. "The mouth a bit puckered. Ears rather prominent. Tight lines from nose to mouth."

"Anything else?" said Mrs. Bott, icily sarcastic.

"I don't think so," said Archie.

Mrs. Bott had risen from her seat. She was breathing heavily.

"I promised to leave it to Vi'let Elizabeth an' I will," she said, "but"—she glared at him in silence for a moment or two, then continued—"if we'd lived in the days of suits of armour an' such like I'd have made Botty fight a *juel* with you, you—you little *toad*!"

Then she turned and swept out of the cottage with as much dignity as her waddling gait allowed, leaving Archie staring after her in mingled mystification and dismay.

She walked back to the Hall, her anger intensified by

a suspicion (which later investigation confirmed) that she had been sitting in a pool of cobalt blue.

But she had no time to worry over the matter. Her annual garden party was to be held next week and more of the "high-ups" had accepted her invitation than had ever accepted it before. Even Sir Gerald and Lady Markham of Marleigh Manor were coming. Mrs. Bott had decided to strain every nerve to make the affair unique in the annals of the village. She played with the idea of dressing the hired waiters in suits of armour, and it took all Mr. Bott's firmness to restrain her from transforming the front of the Hall into a *son et lumière* effect by flood-lighting and gramophone records.

"The light wouldn't show in the daytime, love," he said, "an' no one'd listen an' everyone'll be goin' home about six o'clock."

Reluctantly she yielded and gave her mind to ordering refreshments on an unprecedented scale and devising an ankle-length frock of white lace with a blue silk sash for Violet Elizabeth. Determinedly she put all thought of the portrait out of her mind till the garden party should be over.

So the affair dragged on.

Archie did everything he could think of to better his position. He had another shot at a moustache without any visible results. Then he turned his attention to his car. Tarquin sped over the countryside in a long, sleek, gleaming, purring monster—the latest model of its kind. Archie had a car whose origin was lost in the mists of antiquity. It was battered and dented and shapeless, a number of its vital parts were missing and its paintwork consisted largely of rust. But, despite

"IF WE'D LIVED IN THE DAYS OF SUITS OF ARMOUR I'D HAVE
MADE BOTTY FIGHT A *JUEL* WITH YOU!"

its faults, it was a gallant indomitable little car and
Archie loved it devotedly.

He had to admit, however, that it lacked the touch of
distinction that Tarquin's car undoubtedly possessed
and he decided to do something about it. He stood in
the garage, gazing at it despondently . . . then suddenly
an idea occurred to him. A new coat of paint. His
despondency dropped from him. A new coat of paint
would make all the difference. He bought some green
paint at the oil shop in Hadley and set to work. He
spread it eagerly, generously, over the surface of the
little car. It lay in streaks and blobs. It trickled down

the windscreen, it festooned the windows, it produced a
virulent-looking green rash on the tyres and running-
boards. It failed altogether to adhere to some parts
of the surface. On others it lay thickly in strange and
fantastic patterns. It invaded the inside by way of
holes in the roof, forming designs of daring modernism
on the ancient upholstery.

Archie inspected the final result with a critical frown
and came to the conclusion that it would be improved
by a band of a different colour round the middle. He
decided on pink. He went into Hadley for a tin of pink
paint and set to work again. Archie had not at the
best of times a straight eye and it is possible that the
green paint that covered his nose and eyelashes obscured his vision. But the pink band wandered up and
down in a vague exploratory fashion, vanishing altogether at times to reappear in unexpected places, at
unexpected angles. The lines of worry on Archie's brow
deepened. He couldn't make up his mind whether the
coats of paint were an improvement or not. He kept
going back into his cottage then returning suddenly to
the garage as if to catch his handiwork unawares and
discover what it really looked like. Sometimes it
looked better and sometimes it looked worse.

He decided to start another sketch of Mrs. Bott. He
was desperately anxious to secure the commission. He
was, as usual, short of money. (Archie was always short
of money. He never seemed to spend any and he never
seemed to have any. He didn't know what happened
to it.) But it never occurred to him to try to conciliate
the formidable child in whose hands the decision lay.
And even Tarquin shrank from that humiliating process.

So it was left to the Outlaws and Hubert Lane.

And they all worked hard.

Hubert rang the changes on chocolates, lollypops, sugar mice, jelly babies, caramels and pear drops—and Violet Elizabeth found fault with everything he brought. Still intoxicated by the sense of power, she flung her weight about, tossing her curls, elevating her small nose, keeping him running backwards and forwards to the sweet shop, draining every penny of his pocket money, lavish though it was. Hubert's smug face began to wear an anxious, driven look.

And the Outlaws fared even worse. Ruthlessly Violet Elizabeth organised their games. Where before she had been rigorously excluded, she now lorded it as squaw, exploress, and highwaywoman. She insisted on having the chief part in every game they played. She even forced them to play an outrageous game of her own invention featuring the Outlaws as courtiers and herself as queen.

They endured it till the day before the garden party and then William decided that they could endure it no longer. He summoned a meeting in the old barn.

"We jolly well aren't goin' to have any more of it," he pronounced. "The next time she tries to play with us we'll chase her off same as we used to an'—an' she can scream her head off for all I care."

"Gosh! Hasn't she been awful!" said Ginger. "Wanting to be an exploress an' us the dogs."

"Dogth," mimicked Henry bitterly.

"An' wantin' to be the highwaywoman an' let her tie us to trees."

"Treeth!" said Henry.

"An' whoever heard of a squaw fightin' four pale-faces at once an' scalpin' 'em all?"

"Thcalping!" said Henry.

"Oh, shut up!" said William. His soul revolted from the ignominy of the parts he had been forced to play. "Anyway, we're not doin' it any more. We've *finished* with it."

"But we want Archie to paint the portrait," said Ginger. "He's always been jolly decent to us. We don't want that ole Tarquin Lane to do it."

"No, but we've got to find some other way," said William.

"What way?" said Henry.

"That's what we've got to think out," said William a little testily. "Gosh! We can't think it all out in a second. We've got to make *plans* an' it takes a bit of time to make *plans*."

"Well, I don't see what we can do with Vi'let Elizabeth more than we've been doin' an' we're not goin' to do it any more, so what's left?"

"We've got to find somethin' that'll make Mrs. Bott want Archie to do the portrait," said William. "I bet she's gettin' fed up with Violet Elizabeth, too. If we do somethin' that'll make her want Archie to do it 'stead of that ole Tarquin, I bet she'll leave Violet Elizabeth out of it an' jus' tell him to do it."

"Yes, but what?" said Douglas.

"Oh, shut up!" snapped William. "Why don't you get a bit of thinkin' done 'stead of keep sayin' what? Let's all get a bit of thinkin' done."

They thought in silence for a few moments. The silence was broken by Ginger.

"Gosh! That time she made us play 'Ring-a-ring-o'-rsoes'!"

"Rotheth!" said Henry.

"An' that time she made us crown her Queen of the May!"

"An' that time she made us play an awful game called 'Puss in the Corner'!"

"Puth!" said Henry.

"An' that time she——"

"Oh, shut *up* about it," said William irritably. "We've got to think out this plan. We've not got to waste our brains thinkin' about that rotten ole Violet Elizabeth. Come on. Let's *think*."

There followed another silence, broken only by the heavy breathing that always accompanied the Outlaws' process of thought, till Henry suddenly said:

"He ought to advertise."

"Who?" said Douglas.

"Archie. You can't get anywhere without advertising these days. A man came to dinner at our house last week that worked at an advertising agency and he was talkin' about it. He said it was an age of publicity an' that advertising was the only sure road to success. He said advertising was the street cries of the modern age an' you'd got to shout louder than the next man to make yourself heard. He said an advertisement had to catch the eye and stun the senses. He said you'd got to force your goods on the public if you wanted to sell them."

"Yes, that's an idea," said William. "Gosh! That's a jolly good idea. That's what we'll do. We'll get Archie to advertise an' *force* himself on Mrs. Bott."

"I bet he won't," said Douglas.

"No, p'r'aps he won't," said William, reluctantly facing reality.

"I can't imagine Archie *forcin'* himself on anyone," said Henry.

"He jus' wouldn't know where to start," said Ginger.

"Let's think again, then," said William.

They thought again. Ginger scratched his head. Henry leant his chin on his hand in a Shakespearean attitude. Douglas made ineffectual efforts to catch a fly.

"*Tell* you what!" said William suddenly. "Let's do it for him."

"Do what?" said Douglas, bringing his hand down on his knee and missing the fly again.

"Force him," said William. "If he won't force himself, we'll force him for him."

They considered this in silence.

"How?" said Douglas at least.

"We'll advertise him. We'll make him shout louder than ole Tarquin, same as this man at Henry's said."

"Sounds a bit difficult," said Ginger.

"Oh, yes, start makin' objections," said William with heavy sarcasm. "I've only got to get a good idea for you to start makin' objections. Advertisin'! Gosh, it's as easy as easy. Everyone does it."

"Well, how'll we do it?" said Henry.

"We'll do it same as other people do it," said William a little vaguely.

"How do they?" said Douglas.

"We can't get posters printed about him," said Ginger.

"We can't put him on television," said Henry.

"We can't give free samples of him," said Douglas.

"Oh, shut *up*," said William. "It's Mrs. Bott we've got to advertise him to, so we've jus' got to do the sort of advertisement she likes."

"Well, you don't know what sort she likes."

"Yes, I do," said William. "I've sudd'nly remembered. When she came to tea with my mother once she said that she always got her meat from Hoskyn's in Hadley. She said he was a high-class tradesman an' she liked high-class tradesmen. An' Hoskyn's has an advertisement on his van so we'll put one on Archie's car."

"How?" said Douglas.

"Easy as easy," said William. "Hoskyn's has E. HOSKYNS. BUTCHER. FAMILIES WAITED ON DAILY. So we'll put A. MANNISTER. ARTIST. FAMILIES PAINTED DAILY on Archie's car."

They considered this in silence for a moment or two.

"He wouldn't let us," said Henry at last.

"He'd rub it off if we did," said Ginger.

"I bet he wouldn't even notice it," said William. "He never notices anythin'. An' anyway we'd only have it on for one day. He's goin' to Mrs. Bott's garden party tomorrow so we'll jus' put it on for tomorrow. Then Mrs. Bott'll see it an' she'll be so pleased with it 'cause of it bein' a high-class advertisement that she'll fix up with him to do this portrait right away. An' I bet it'll make everyone else at the garden party want him to do theirs. It's a jolly good idea."

"It'll make an awful mess of his car," said Henry thoughtfully.

"He's made a mess of it himself to start with," said William. "It's a good thing he has, too. It'll set people off lookin' at it, then they'll see the advertisement an' it'll make them want him to paint them."

"When shall we do it?" said Ginger.

"Well, the garden party's tomorrow afternoon, so let's do it tomorrow mornin'," said William. His ever-ready optimism rose in a flood. "Gosh! It's all settled now. He'll paint Mrs. Bott's portrait an' we'll have got rid of that ole Violet Elizabeth for good."

"Time will show," said Douglas with a touch of cynicism in his voice.

They approached Archie's cottage warily the next morning and stood in the shelter of the hedge inspecting it.

"He's in," whispered Ginger. "I can see him."

"Shut up!" hissed William. "He's jus' comin' out."

Archie emerged from the cottage with a little pile of books under his arm. They realised that he was going to the Library. There was a small and somewhat antiquated "Art Section" in Hadley Public Library and Archie was conscientiously plodding his way through it. They watched him till he was out of sight, then entered the gate and approached the garage. The garage doors were fitted with lock and key, but responded to the simple device of pushing one door, whereupon the catch slid out of the lock and both doors opened. William pushed the door. It opened. The Outlaws entered. The vivid green and the wandering pink band were somewhat startling in the semi-darkness of the garage. They blinked for a moment, dazzled by the sight.

"Well, he's backed it in, anyway," said William. "That's one good thing. He'll only see the front when he gets in."

Archie found the process of backing his car into the main road a difficult and nerve-racking one (racking the nerves not only of Archie himself but of all the passers-by) so he made a rule of backing it into the garage when he put it away. This too was a lengthy and difficult process, involving much wear and tear of both car and garage, but he generally managed it in the end.

The four went round to the rear of the car and examined it.

"There's room for the advertisement here," said
William, pointing to the space above the window. "It'll
go in easy."

"What'll we do it with?" said Ginger.

"Let's have a look in his cottage an' see if we can
find anythin'," said William.

They trooped into Archie's cottage and wandered
about among the litter that covered the rooms. It
was William who found the tin of shoe blacking in a
cullender on the draining board in the kitchen.

"I bet this'd do," he said. "Let's have a try, anyway."

They returned to the garage. William dug his finger
into the tin and wrote "Archie Mannister Artist" across
the back of the car. The first attempt was thin and
ghost-like.

"Try again an' do it thicker," suggested Henry.

William tried again and did it thicker—did it thicker
and thicker till the lettering (if somewhat erratic)
showed black and shiny. He completed the advertisement then stepped back to inspect the result. It
sprawled drunkenly across the green paint.

ARCHIE MANNISTER ARTIST FAMMILYS
PAYNTED DAYLY.

"I think it looks jolly good," he said. "It's high
class, anyway, so I bet Mrs. Bott'll like it."

"There's a picture of a cow on Hoskyn's van,"
Ginger reminded him.

"Gosh, yes! So there is!" said William. "I'd forgotten that. Well, let's get one of Archie's pictures an'
stick it on. Come along! Let's go'n' find one."

"I THINK IT LOOKS JOLLY GOOD," SAID WILLIAM. "IT'S HIGH
CLASS, ANYWAY."

They returned to the studio. Canvasses stood stacked
against the wall. Chairs and tables were covered with
half-finished sketches. A collection of ancient tattered
engravings that Archie had bought at Marsh's junk
shop the day before lay scattered about the floor.

William picked up one of the sketches. It was
Archie's second attempt at Mrs. Bott. It looked less
like Mr. Pickwick but less like Mrs. Bott.

"Gosh!" he said excitedly. "It's got Mrs. Bott's
name written underneath. We'll stick *this* on. I bet
she'll be jolly pleased with it."

Ginger had taken up a small canvas that represented

one of Archie's less fortunate efforts at "modern art."
It consisted in a confusion of geometrical shapes with
what looked like a grasshopper holding up an umbrella
in one corner and what looked like a washing machine
in another.

"Let's put this on," he said. "It'll catch the eye an'
stun the senses all right."

"Gosh, yes!" said Henry. He took up one of the
engravings. "An' let's have this, too. It's a house.
It'll show he can draw houses." He examined the engraving with a critical frown. "He's drawn it jolly
well, too. All these tiny little lines. . . ."

"Come on," said William. "Let's start on 'em. He'll
be comin' back before we've finished if we're not quick.
Let's find some sticking stuff."

Henry found a roll of "sticking stuff" at the

bottom of a jar marked "Sugar" on the chimney-piece and they returned to the garage and set to work again.

The sketch of Mrs. Bott and the canvas fitted excellently on either side of the rear window with the engraving just beneath.

Douglas kept watch at the gate.

"He's comin'," he shouted suddenly as he saw Archie turning into the lane, carrying "History of Medieval Art" and "Great Victorian Painters" under his arm.

Henry stuck down the last corner of the engraving and the four crept furtively out through a gap in the hedge and made their way home.

"I bet he'll take it off before he goes to the party," said Douglas.

"I bet he won't even notice it," said William.

And William was right.

Archie didn't even notice it.

He was a little later starting out than he had meant to be as he forgot to change into his suit till the last minute and then couldn't find it. (Archie wore his suit so seldom that he could never remember where he kept it.) After a lengthy search he remembered that he had put it under the carpet in his bedroom some weeks ago to get the creases out. He retrieved it, shook the dust from it, changed into it hastily, went to the garage and climbed into the driving seat.

The little car started up easily and he drove off to Mrs. Bott's garden party with no thought in his mind but the obtaining of the commission to paint her portrait.

He entered the drive of the Hall and drew up his car behind the Rolls Royce in which Sir Gerald and Lady Markham had just arrived. Behind him there drew up the Daimler that contained Sir Gervase and Lady Torrance of Steedham Grange. Archie dismounted from his car (he failed to notice that the occupants of the Daimler still sat there as if paralysed, their eyes fixed in incredulous horror on the back of his car) and made his way round the house to the lawn.

The festivities were at their height. Ices and straw-berries and cream were being handed round among the guests. Strains of the ballet music from *Faust* floated out from the bandstand on the terrace. The more adventurous of the guests were playing clock golf and quoits. The others stood about in groups talking. Everyone seemed happy and cheerful. Only Mrs. Bott's brow was clouded. For Violet Elizabeth was not there. The ankle-length frock with the blue silk sash still hung in the white-painted wardrobe. And Violet Elizabeth lay in bed, a victim to the worst bilious attack that had ever racked that fairy-like form. Mrs. Bott, going to her bedroom before breakfast, had found her in the throes of it and on the floor by the bed the empty chocolate box that Hubert had brought her the evening before. It was the largest and most expensive he had ever brought, for he had decided to clinch the matter of the portrait once and for all before the garden party ended. Violet Elizabeth admitted—between bouts—that she had awakened early and consumed the whole boxful in one operation.

"Hubert Lane gave it me," she said weakly. "He'th a nathty boy. I hope he'll be thorry when I'm dead. I feel ath if I wath going to die quite thoon now."

"No, you're not goin' to die, love," Mrs. Bott reassured her. "The doctor'll give you some nice medicine and you'll soon be all right."

"I've felt ill for dayth an' *dayth*," said Violet Elizabeth plaintively. "He *keepth* giving me chocolatth and thingth. I can't *thtop* him. He'th a horrid boy. I think he wanth to poithon me."

"Now you lie still, love," said Mrs. Bott. Her face grew grim. "That Tarquin's at the bottom of it, I shouldn't be surprised. I might have known he was up to no good with a moustache like that. Snake in the grass, that's what he is. Seems I'll have to have Archie Mannister for that portrait, after all."

When Tarquin arrived at the party he was surprised by the chilliness of his reception and the icy glare fixed on him by his hostess. Archie, arriving a few minutes later, was equally surprised (and not a little embarrassed) by the warmth of Mrs. Bott's handclasp and the width of her smile.

"Now, 'ave a good time," she said. "A nice game of clock golf, or somethin'. I'm just goin' up to see 'ow pore little Vi'let Elizabeth is."

Violet Elizabeth was feeling a little better. But suffering had not had a chastening effect on her. Already her self-expression had taken the form of hurling her bottle of medicine out of the open window. Mr. Bott had gone to the doctor's for another bottle and his wife had a dark and well-founded suspicion that he intended to prolong the expedition as much as possible in order to provide himself with an alibi for staying away from the garden party.

"Now let me 'ave a nice little take at your temperature, love," she coaxed.

"Go away!" stormed Violet Elizabeth. "If you don't go away, I'll thcream an' I'll thcream an' I'll thcream till

I'm thick," adding with a touch of complacency, "I can be thick thpecially eathily juth now."

Defeated, Mrs. Bott returned to her guests and it was as she was descending the stairs that she caught sight of the back of Archie's car from the landing window. Her little round face grew purple. Her small eyes nearly popped out of her head. Her breathing resembled that of an infuriated bull. As quickly as her plump little figure could move, it made its way down the stairs and through the crowd on the lawn to Archie. She stood for a moment, breathing at him, searching for words.

"'Ow—'ow—'ow *dare* you?" she said at last.

Archie stared at her in mute bewilderment.

"'Ow *dare* you?" she repeated, on a higher note.

"I—I don't know what you mean," said Archie, blinking distractedly.

Mrs. Bott's words still seemed to come with difficulty.

"Your car . . ." she managed to get out. "Your car . . ."

Archie continued to gaze at her in mute bewilderment for a few moments, then enlightenment seemed to come. He had himself grown accustomed to his car but he realised suddenly that it might cut a poor figure beside the Rolls Royces and Daimlers in which her other guests had arrived. A certain dignity invaded his manner.

"I'm sorry you don't like it," he said.

"Like it!?" almost screamed Mrs. Bott.

"It was a good make of car originally," said Archie distantly, "and it still gives what I consider a good performance." He paused and added with a burst of honesty, "At times."

"It's not the car itself as you well know," said Mrs. Bott. "It's what you've 'ad the imperdence to put on it."

Archie considered what he had put on it.

"I think the colours blend quite well together," he said. "I admit that the pink has run in places and actually the green paint in the tin was of an odd consistency—liquid at the top and solid at the bottom—but the general effect, I consider, is not unpleasant."

"Not——!" choked Mrs. Bott. "It's what you've put on the *back* I'm talkin' about, you imperdent puppy! 'Ow *dare* you!"

Archie remembered the streaks of green and pink paint that obscured the rear window but decided to stick to his guns.

"I consider I made a very good job of the back," he said. "A modern and up-to-date job. I realize that the scheme is essentially modern and that old-fashioned people may not like it, but——"

"It's libel, that's what it is," said Mrs. Bott. She was gobbling like an enraged turkey cock. "It's libel an' slander an' insult an' imperdence an'—an' I'm goin' to fetch the police to it this very minute."

"I don't know what you mean," said Archie.

The guests had gathered round. Sir Gerald and Lady Markham were looking with concern and dismay from Archie to their hostess.

"Let's go and have a look at the thing," suggested Sir Gerald. "There may be some mistake."

Led by Mrs. Bott and Archie, the guests surged round the house and congregated at the back of the car.

"Look!" said Mrs. Bott, pointing a plump trembling finger at the "advertisement." "Look at that and deny it if you can, you—you saucy little 'ound-*H*ound!"

Archie looked at it. His mouth dropped open. He stared frantically in front of him as if in the grip of a nightmare.

"'Ow you 'ad the *nerve!*" said Mrs. Bott in a voice that quavered with emotion.

"I didn't! I didn't!" protested Archie wildly. "I've never seen it till this moment." His voice had risen to a sort of bleat. "I swear I haven't."

"Well, 'oo did it if you didn't?" said Mrs. Bott.

"I don't know," bleated Archie, running his hands through his hair. "I just don't *know*."

Mrs. Bott's eyes shot round the group and came to rest on Tarquin. Tarquin was watching the scene with a malicious smile.

"And what are you grinning at, you young jacka-napes?" she flamed. "You aren't much better. Poison-ing the pore child's stomach with cheap chocolates."

"Me?" said the outraged Tarquin. "I've never given the wretched child a chocolate in my life."

"'Wretched child!'" echoed Mrs. Bott shrilly. "Pore little suffering angel! Well, you've cooked *your* goose, young man. I wouldn't be seen dead bein' painted by you now."

"And I wouldn't be seen dead painting you," said Tarquin loftily. "So the matter is settled to our mutual satisfaction."

He gave a twirl to his moustache and set off with slow dignity down the drive.

Archie was still grappling with his nightmare.

"I don't know how it *got* there," he wailed, his eyes still fixed in fascinated horror on the decorations that covered his car.

"Some ill-advised practical joke," said Sir Gerald

ARCHIE'S MOUTH DROPPED OPEN. HE STARED FRANTICALLY IN
FRONT OF HIM AS IF IN THE GRIP OF A NIGHTMARE.

easily. "Don't worry, my boy. No one would for a
moment suppose that you were responsible for it."

"Oh, wouldn't they!" said Mrs. Bott aggressively.
"Well, let me tell you——"

"Gerald!" called Lady Markham excitedly.

She was examining the engraving that Henry had
fixed beneath the rear window.

"Yes, my dear?"

"Come and look at this. It's an engraving of the
Manor before your great-grandfather made the al-

terations. We knew there was an engraving of it but we've never been able to find a copy. We've hunted and advertised and asked people . . . Oh, look at it, Gerald! Here's the ornamental fountain on the lawn. I knew there was one—I think someone brought it home from Italy—but I never could think what it looked like. It's charming. . . . And the gabled frontage of the house, before your great-grandfather put up the pseudo-Palladian one. Oh, it's *wonderful!*" She turned to Archie. "Does it belong to you?"

"Yes," said Archie, "but"—his voice rose to a wail again—"I don't know how it *got* there."

"Never mind that. May we buy it from you?"

"Yes, certainly," stammered Archie. "I gave five bob for the lot at Marsh's. It'll probably work out at about twopence."

"Oh, but of *course* we'll pay you more than that," said Lady Markham. "We can discuss it later. You see, it's really *valuable* to us. You must understand that it's really valuable to us. It's probably the only copy in existence and we've hunted for it for years."

There was a deprecating note in her voice as if she were apologising for the handsome price she intended to pay him.

"Well, it's cured me of portraits, anyway," said Mrs. Bott. "It's cured me of portraits for good and all. If you've got to go through all this to get your portrait took—well, it's wore me out before it's started."

Lady Markham patted her shoulder reassuringly, then turned again to Archie. Something wistful in his thin, harassed-looking face touched her heart.

"Do you paint gardens?" she said.

Archie brightened. He almost glowed. For Archie was a dab at gardens. Nothing could ever be redder than his roses, bluer than his delphiniums, greener than his grass.

"Oh, yes," he said eagerly. "Yes, indeed."

"Well, you must come and paint mine," said Lady Markham, "and I'll have it made into a Christmas card."

"Oh, thank you, *thank* you," said Archie gratefully.

"Yes, I'm through with portraits," said Mrs. Bott. Her anger, though fiery, was short-lived and already was fading into a plaintive melancholy. "I couldn't 'ave stood the strain of it. I'm too 'igh strung. It'd've drove me mental inside of a week. No, I won't 'ave no more portraits—*h*ave—but"—her face lit up suddenly—"I'll 'ave an ornamental founting on the lawn instead.

Same as in the picture. That's what I'll do. An ornamental founting on the lawn."

"You can have the one in the engraving copied if you
like," said Lady Markham.

"Thank you," said Mrs. Bott. "That'd do me a
treat. . . . Now let's all go back an' get on with the
party."

But Archie felt that—in his case, at any rate—it
would be an anticlimax. He was still bewildered, still
shaken, still racked by emotion. He took his farewell
of Mrs. Bott, got into the little car, turned it round in
the drive by what seemed a miracle and drove out of the
gate.

William, Ginger, Henry and Douglas were waiting
in the road. He stopped the car.

"Can I give you boys a lift?" he said.

They clambered into the car. After a long and noisy
tussle with it Archie got it started again. It reversed
unexpectedly, then shot forward down the road.

"Was it all right, Archie?" said William anxiously.
"Is she goin' to let you paint her portrait?"

"No," said Archie. "Some fool messed up the back
of my car."

"It was me," said William in a small voice.

"It was all of us," chorused Ginger, Henry and
Douglas.

"We did it for the best," said Ginger.

"Publicity is the only sure road to success," said
Henry. "The street cries of the modern world."

"We thought it would help you," said Douglas.

Archie gave his thin reedy laugh.

"Well, actually, it did," he said.

"Tell us about it, Archie," they clamoured.

He told them about it.

"But that's *smashing*, Archie," said William.

"Well, yes, it is rather—smashing," said Archie. "And I'd much rather paint gardens than people. You know where you are with them."

"Look out!" said William as the little car tried to climb the bank into the hedge at a bend of the road.

After a short tussle with Archie, it climbed down, reversed for some yards, then shot forward again down the road.

The bend in the road had brought Tarquin's figure into view. The little car made as if to butt him playfully in the back, then thought better of it and stopped abruptly. Archie tried the starting button without success, then got out and tried the starting handle, still without success.

"Can I give a hand?" said Tarquin.

They flooded the carburettor and swung the handle in turns. Nothing happened. Then Archie took hold of the car and shook it violently. Everything in it rattled and it started up suddenly.

"It does that sometimes," he explained.

"You'd better get in while the going's good," said Tarquin. He held out his hand. Archie grasped it. "We're both well out of that portrait business, old chap."

Archie gave his simple ingenuous smile.

"We are indeed," he said.

"Good luck!" said Tarquin as Archie leapt just in time into the little car, which had started off at a break-neck speed of its own accord.

The next bend in the road brought Hubert into view. As they passed him, William leant out of the window

and pulled his Face. Hubert pulled his own Face back.
There was no malice in the exchange. It was simply a
display of craftsmanship by brother artists. Hubert's
Face was not in the same class as William's (William's
Face had made strong men blench), but, as William
generously admitted to himself, it wasn't bad. For a
fleeting moment he was almost tempted to wave to him,
but he resisted the temptation. Life without Hubert
as an enemy would be unendurably dull.

"I can hardly believe it," said Archie, dreamily.
"Getting paid for the engraving and getting a commission for painting the garden. . . ."

They had reached Archie's cottage now. The little
car hesitated, seemed about to race on down the road,
then changed its mind, charged through the gate, performed a couple of full circles on the lawn then backed
decorously into its garage.